RANDOM ACTS OF OUTRAGE

HOLLY ANNA PALADIN MYSTERIES, BOOK 6

CHRISTY BARRITT

River Heights

COMPLETE BOOK LIST

Squeaky Clean Mysteries:

#13 Cold Case: Clean Getaway

#14 Cold Case: Clean Sweep

While You Were Sweeping, A Riley Thomas Spinoff

The Sierra Files:

#1 Pounced

#2 Hunted

#3 Pranced

#4 Rattled

#5 Caged (coming soon)

The Gabby St. Claire Diaries (a Tween Mystery series):

The Curtain Call Caper

The Disappearing Dog Dilemma

The Bungled Bike Burglaries

The Worst Detective Ever

#1 Ready to Fumble

#2 Reign of Error

#3 Safety in Blunders

#4 Join the Flub

#5 Blooper Freak

#6 Flaw Abiding Citizen

#7 Gaffe Out Loud (coming soon)

#8 Joke and Dagger (coming soon)

Raven Remington

Relentless 1

Relentless 2 (coming soon)

Holly Anna Paladin Mysteries:

#1 Random Acts of Murder

#2 Random Acts of Deceit

#2.5 Random Acts of Scrooge

#3 Random Acts of Malice

#4 Random Acts of Greed

#5 Random Acts of Fraud

#6 Random Acts of Outrage

#7 Random Acts of Iniquity (coming soon)

Lantern Beach Mysteries

#1 Hidden Currents

#2 Flood Watch

#3 Storm Surge

#4 Dangerous Waters

#5 Perilous Riptide

#6 Deadly Undertow

Lantern Beach Romantic Suspense

Tides of Deception

Shadow of Intrigue (coming soon)

Storm of Doubt (coming soon)

Carolina Moon Series:
Home Before Dark
Gone By Dark
Wait Until Dark
Light the Dark
Taken By Dark

Suburban Sleuth Mysteries:
Death of the Couch Potato's Wife

Cape Thomas Series:
Dubiosity
Disillusioned
Distorted

Standalone Romantic Mystery:
The Good Girl

Suspense:
Imperfect
The Wrecking

Standalone Romantic-Suspense:
Keeping Guard
The Last Target
Race Against Time
Ricochet

Key Witness

Lifeline

High-Stakes Holiday Reunion

Desperate Measures

Hidden Agenda

Mountain Hideaway

Dark Harbor

Shadow of Suspicion

The Baby Assignment

Nonfiction:

Characters in the Kitchen

Changed: True Stories of Finding God through Christian Music (out of print)

The Novel in Me: The Beginner's Guide to Writing and Publishing a Novel (out of print)

CHAPTER 1

I CAST a steely gaze at my opponent and lowered my voice. "You will not defeat me."

My to-do list stared back, nearly mocking me with its impossible length. It was like my responsibilities had teamed up on me and knew I had no time. Now, they were delighting in making me feel guilty and inadequate.

I leaned back into the seat of my baby blue, vintage Mustang and closed my eyes. The rain pitter-pattered against my rooftop, the sound soothing to my frazzled soul.

I was trying to get a grasp on this whole balance thing, but it was more difficult than all those self-help magazine articles made it seem. I was essentially trying to be a full-time working single mom. I was twenty-nine, I'd never been married, and I'd never given birth.

It had been a baptism by fire.

I thought with my organizational skills, experience as a social worker, and God-given instincts that I'd be a natural at parenting.

I wasn't.

But I had left work just in time to pick up Sarah, and I'd celebrate the small victories by checking that off my list.

Sarah was my newest foster daughter. She'd been at my house for the past two months, and I could sense something resilient in her. It gave me hope that she was going to rise above all the challenges in her life and succeed. All she needed was a little support and encouragement.

She was in ninth grade, and she'd captured my heart on the first night she stayed with me when she'd recognized that I was playing Ella Fitzgerald. I'd liked her ever since.

My phone rang, and I saw it was Drew Williams, my new boyfriend. And, by new, I meant we'd been dating for six months. Six *wonderful* months.

"Hey, beautiful." His smooth voice rolled across the line. "How was your day?"

I warmed just hearing him. Drew was so good to me. Everyone said we were well-suited for each other, and I had to agree. We seemed like a perfect match. In fact, we hadn't even had a fight since we got together. That was a sign, right? Something to check off my list of admirable qualities to look for in a future spouse.

Drew had asked me about my day, I remembered.

"It's been okay," I said, remembering the endless phone calls I'd endured while working as a community liaison for my brother, Ralph, a state senator. "Actually, it's been stressful. Lots of work and lots of people calling in unhappy."

"You could work in my profession. None of my clients speak to me."

Drew was a mortician, a job that I couldn't even begin to wrap my idealistic mind around. Death and grief were not something I wanted to surround myself with. "Very funny. Working with the families of the deceased is no easy task, and don't tell me it is."

"You'll get no argument from me. Listen, do you and Sarah want to come over tonight? I thought we could have a cookout. Maybe have a bonfire with some hotdogs."

"That sounds fun. Throw in some s'mores, and we'll never want to leave."

He chuckled. "I'd be okay with that. I'll see the two of you at six, then."

I smiled at his words. Drew was going to be a wonderful family man one day. "Sounds great."

"Love you, Holly."

My breath caught at his words. It wasn't the first time

Drew had declared his love for me, but I hadn't been able to return the sentiment. That fact made me feel like an absolute failure in the commitment department. But I couldn't say those words unless I was certain they were true.

After six months, you'd think I'd be sure, right?

My best friend, Jamie, certainly thought that. As she should. She spoke aloud the thoughts lingering in the back of my mind that I didn't dare release into the world.

Everyone needed a friend like her.

"I lo . . . ook forward to seeing you later."

I sighed as I pulled up two spaces in the carpool lane. *Lame, Holly. Lame.*

I could let Sarah ride the bus. But the girl already had so many things thrown at her. Her life had been in an upheaval for a while now, and I didn't want to add any additional stress.

So I'd decided I would drop her off and pick her up from school every day.

However, I'd arrived a good ten minutes early—I hadn't hit any red lights. So I had some time to kill.

As I sat there, I started to scroll through some old pictures I'd saved on my phone. I'd been resistant to using my cell for anything but phone calls and a few pictures until lately. Now I'd become reliant on the device, and part of me hated myself for it. Learning information about friends face-to-face—sharing life that way—

was so much better. But the world around me didn't agree.

I paused when I came to a picture from last year at this time.

My heart panged.

It was a picture of me with Chase Dexter, my former boyfriend, at a charity gala my mom had organized— Chase in his tux and me in a lovely rose-gold gown. And we looked so happy as we smiled at the camera, a blur of string lights creating a magical background behind us.

How had things changed so quickly? How had our forever together turned into never together?

I turned off my phone and frowned.

That was life. There was no use lamenting about the past. Decisions had been made, and I could do nothing to change them. Nope, I'd learn from my mistakes and move on. But, if I was honest with myself, I knew my grief still remained, despite my logic. One didn't easily move past losing the person assumed to be your soulmate.

Finally, the line started moving forward in front of the school, where students lingered with backpacks slung over their shoulders and impatient expressions on their faces. I'd pick up Sarah, take her back to my place to do her homework, and then we'd head to Drew's.

It sounded like the perfect day.

The cars ahead of me moved up, students jumping inside before the drivers pulled away. Car after car picked up their children until I was at the front of the line, and all the vehicles behind me had to go around.

What in the world was taking Sarah so long? She was usually one of the first students out.

The gray and rainy day made it harder to see through the windows. Maybe Sarah was waiting inside, out of the dampness, until she saw me. I hadn't sent her with an umbrella, after all. Foster mom fail number 52. Then again, she should recognize this Mustang anywhere.

The beginnings of panic started inside me, but I pushed it down. This was just a misunderstanding. Sarah was inside waiting, and she would come out in a few minutes and hop into my car, just like she did five days a week. I'd laugh at myself for being so paranoid.

My hands felt clammy, though.

I resisted the urge to check my phone to pass the time. I could wait this out.

Until I realized there were no more cars behind me and that everyone else had come and gone.

Okay, I was going to need to go inside. Maybe there was some kind of miscommunication, and maybe Sarah was staying after for some reason. Had she joined a club? It seemed unlikely, but I needed a reason not to freak out and that seemed like a good one.

I pulled into a parking space, grabbed my purse, and darted through the rain into the building.

I'd halfway expected to see Sarah there, waiting for

me or rushing to the door, claiming she'd lost track of time.

But she wasn't.

I pictured her in my mind. Sarah's mom was Hispanic and her dad Caucasian, which left Sarah with a beautiful skin tone. She had dark hair that she wore long—nearly to her waist. She was petite and thin and curious. While some of the kids I'd fostered had been defiant, Sarah had been quiet and studious.

And not like the type to be MIA at pickup.

I hurried to the office and talked to the woman at the front desk, who gave me a curious glance, one that clearly stated she thought I might be overreacting. "The only clubs meeting after school today, besides our sports teams, are the French Club and the Robotics Club. Is she a part of either of those?"

"No, she doesn't take French classes, and she can't even work the remote for my TV most of the time." Neither seemed like a distant possibility even.

"Maybe she went home with a friend?"

"I don't think she'd do that."

"Does she have a cell phone?"

I shook my head, anxiety still climbing inside me. "No, she doesn't. I would have called her if she did."

The woman frowned and tapped her French-tipped nails against the laminate countertop. "Let me see what I can find out. Excuse me a minute."

After she walked away, I searched through my cell contacts until I found the numbers of some of Sarah's friends. I called the two I had, but both said Sarah mentioned getting picked up by me and they didn't know anything else.

What had happened between her last class and now?

The administrative assistant came back a minute later —without Sarah again. "Ms. Paladin, I'm not sure what's going on. Sarah doesn't appear to be here at the school, though. I called down to the club coordinator, and no one has seen her."

"I just called two of her friends, and they said she came toward the office for pickup." My panic kicked up a notch, even though I tried to hold it back. "Listen, could I talk to Principal Hamlin?"

The principal, a fifty-something woman with super-short blonde hair and a round face, emerged from a back office a few minutes later. Her expression made it clear that she'd been apprised on what had happened.

"Ms. Paladin." She paused in front of me and clasped her hands together. "I understand that your foster daughter didn't meet you after school and you're concerned about this."

"Can I talk to the teacher who dismissed her at the end of the day? Something just feels wrong about all of this."

"Of course. I'll call her down."

"Thank you." I crossed my arms and tried to remain in control of my emotions. But I was a quivering mess inside.

No, don't go there, Holly. Don't go to the place where you imagine Sarah being scared and alone. There's probably a good explanation for this. You'll have a good laugh later and chide yourself for overreacting.

Ms. Baldwin, Sarah's last-period teacher, showed up a minute later and hurried over to me. The petite young teacher had hair so blonde it was almost white, and right now she looked wired.

We'd met during open house. Then we'd kind of hit it off and had met later for coffee. Ms. Baldwin, also single, was considering being a foster mom, and we'd talked for a good two hours about it. She was the kind of teacher who went the extra mile for her students, and I had to admire that.

"I just heard you're looking for Sarah," she rushed. "I saw her walking toward the student parking lot."

I swallowed hard, certain I hadn't heard correctly. "What?"

"A woman pulled up. I didn't think anything of it. You know Sarah has had numerous foster moms over the past six months. I couldn't remember . . ." Her voice cracked, and she looked away.

"You saw her get into the car with another woman?" I repeated, making sure I'd heard correctly.

She nodded nervously. "That's right. I did. I'm so sorry. Sarah is *such* a good girl. I hope this is all just a misunderstanding."

"We need to call Detective Chase Dexter. Now. Sarah has Type 1 diabetes. If she doesn't manage it correctly . . ." I swallowed hard. "Well, it could be fatal."

CHAPTER 2

I PACED to the corner of the school office for some privacy, my cell phone stuck to my ear as I talked to the social worker who'd been assigned to Sarah. Kathy Langston had no idea who would have picked Sarah up, but she was going to look into it. As soon as I ended the call with her, I called Sarah's previous foster mom, Erin. The two of us had kept in touch as a means of support, especially about Sarah's diabetes.

Erin hadn't heard from Sarah either but promised to be in touch if she did.

With each passing moment and each phone call, my anxiety grew.

Something was seriously wrong here.

Sarah had problems, but I couldn't see her getting in the car with someone else without mentioning it to me.

Then again, some of these kids in the foster care system had more problems than I could ever fathom. Their trust and attachment issues were something that I thought I could grasp, but, unless I was in their shoes, I knew I really couldn't.

Trauma changed the way people's brains worked and the way their internal processing systems operated. But my goal was to ensure these kids didn't get lost in the cracks. To give them someone to fall back on.

And I felt like a failure right now.

"Holly?"

At the sound of the voice, my entire body tensed.

I knew who had called me without looking. But my lungs still froze, and time felt suspended.

It had been six months since I'd seen Chase.

I knew this moment would come, the moment where the two of us would run into each other again. But I hadn't been able to fully prepare for the encounter—not emotionally, at least.

Plastering on a smile, I slowly turned, ready to put on a show—one that proclaimed I was doing great since our breakup.

Instead, my heart turned into a puddle when I saw him.

Chase.

My Chase.

Except he wasn't my Chase anymore.

He was my ex, and he was off limits.

"Chase . . ." I finally pulled myself together long enough to speak. The show I'd envisioned putting on wasn't happening right now. Which was fine because fake wasn't really my thing. Sometimes that worked to my detriment. "Thanks so much for coming."

I wanted to step into his arms. To tell him I'd missed him. To feel one of his all-consuming bear hugs that assured me everything would be okay like only Chase could do.

But I couldn't do that.

Chase wasn't ready for a long-term relationship. And I couldn't keep dating him knowing he was stringing me along. I wanted to be a mom and a wife. I was ready for that next step in life.

Chase wasn't.

End of story. Our two paths didn't meet at the end.

I'd taken the figurative bull by the horns and paved my own way. I'd bought my own place. Become a foster mom. And I'd met Drew.

"You look good, Holly." Chase's eyes were warm and captivating and seemed to hypnotize me with their depths.

I did a little curtsy in my A-line dress. "Thank you."

Chase looked good also. I'd always thought he looked like Chris Hemsworth. The former football player still maintained his pro athlete physique. But echoes of

Chase's past haunted his gaze like ghosts at a beautiful cemetery.

"What's going on?" he asked. "The school called about a student. And, based on the look on your face, you're in the middle of this."

I snapped back to the moment, my cheeks heating as I realized I'd gotten distracted by man drama, even if it was for only two minutes. How could I have forgotten about Sarah so easily?

I hadn't. I really hadn't. But seeing Chase had shaken me up.

"My new foster daughter . . ." My throat ached as the words tried to leave my lips. "I came to pick her up only to find out someone else already had. Her name is Sarah Anderson."

"No one else ever picks her up?"

I shook my head. "No, and I already called the social worker as well as her old foster mom and two of her friends."

"How about her birth parents? Are they in the picture?"

"No, the dad is in jail and the mom is MIA. Has been for seven years. Kathy—the social worker—is going to look into them, just in case."

"Cameras?"

"The principal is pulling up the footage from the parking lot as we speak."

Chase stepped closer and squeezed my arm, obviously sensing my distress. I could hear the thinness in my voice, and I knew my motions were jerky.

Sarah wasn't my flesh and blood, but I was responsible for her. I cared about her, and the thought of anything bad happening to her . . . well, I just couldn't handle it.

"I'm going to do everything I can to find her, Holly," Chase said.

"Thank you." My voice cracked as I said the words.

Please, Lord, let her be okay.

CHAPTER 3

I STOOD behind the principal and Chase as they sat at a desk and reviewed the camera footage from the parking lot after school today. The dreary day made the video blurry and hard to make out.

Sure enough, a sedan pulled up to the curb by the student lot, where Sarah waited with her backpack.

My eyes were fixated on the screen, and I could hardly breathe as I waited to see what happened.

Sarah stepped near the car. Leaned inside the passenger door window for a minute, as if talking to the driver. The next moment, she got inside.

She got *inside*.

She didn't appear to be distressed or upset. No, it was almost like she knew the person.

What were you thinking, Wonder Girl? That was my nickname for Sarah because I always told her she could do anything she set her mind to. That she could be anyone she desired to be. All it took was hard work and determination.

"I'll run the license plate," Chase said. "This may not be an abduction, however. We need to consider that maybe Sarah just left. Foster kids have run away before."

"Not Sarah." I crossed my arms. "She wouldn't do that."

"It's just something we need to consider. Either way, we'll still search for her."

"Maybe you could talk to more of her friends. Maybe she said something to them."

"We'll see what we can find out, Holly." Chase said the words calmly, like a hostage negotiator trying to deescalate a situation.

I knew he was capable. It was just that . . . life could change in the blink of an eye, and there were no super humans who could stop it—no matter how strong, smart, or capable they were.

"Holly?"

I twirled around. Drew stood in the doorway of the office, and I flew into his arms. He pulled me close, and I finally got the embrace I'd been longing for. With my boyfriend. Not my ex. The way it should be.

"How are you?" Drew murmured in my ear.

I remembered that Chase was watching us, and self-consciousness hit me so hard it felt like an oversized 1950s etiquette book had been dropped on my head. I pulled back and straightened my dress. PDA wasn't my thing. And PDA with my current boyfriend in front of my ex-boyfriend? Definitely not kosher or ladylike.

"I've been better," I said.

Drew's gaze hit behind me, and his eyes frosted ever-so-slightly as he nodded. "Chase."

Chase nodded back, just as stiffly. "Drew."

Before the men could stare each other down any longer, I took Drew's arm and led him away from the room. He was dressed in his customary suit and tie—his work uniform as a funeral home director and mortician.

His wavy dark hair was combed back away from his face, and his chiseled features and olive skin looked polished and debonair. No doubt about it, the man was handsome. And a gentleman. And always there for me when I needed him.

"I didn't know you were coming," I said. I'd called him shortly before Chase arrived, while I'd been waiting to hear back from one of Sarah's friends.

"Of course I came." He squeezed my arm. "I didn't want you to go through this alone."

"Thank you. I appreciate it. You're always good to

me." I said that a lot. But Drew really *was* good to me, so much so that I almost felt unworthy.

He pulled me into another hug, this one out of sight from anyone else. "I just can't believe Sarah is missing."

"Neither can I."

"How about if I get you back home? The police can handle it from here." He started to tug me away.

I froze, every part of me rebelling at the thought. "I can't leave, Drew."

"It looks like everything is being taken care of." He started to tug me again.

I didn't budge, and nothing would change that. "But the police might need my input."

"Then he—they—can call you."

"I'd prefer to be here."

Drew paused. He didn't sigh, but I could sense that he wanted to. Whenever we did have our first fight, it would probably be because, beneath my prim and proper ideals, I was strong-willed and stubborn. "Okay then. If you feel better staying then we'll stay."

We'll stay? I wasn't sure that having Drew here would actually help this situation. But I didn't know how to put it delicately. So I clamped my mouth shut instead until I could think of something else to talk about.

"I'm going to try and call more of Sarah's friends," I said. "Maybe they heard something."

"I could put together a prayer chain."

My heart melted just a little. "You'd do that?"

"Of course. Anything you need, I'm here."

I nodded as a plan began forming in my mind. "That's a great idea. Go ahead and call members of our small group, if you don't mind, and ask them to pray. I'm going to plan a family meeting tonight. If we put all of our heads together, maybe we can figure this out. I want you to come. Of course."

"I'll be there. But . . . are you sure you're okay here by yourself?" He glanced behind me, to the room where I'd left Chase.

"I'll be fine. I just don't feel right leaving yet. I'll call you when I do."

When Drew disappeared out of sight, I felt an unusual weight of relief. I wanted to put all of my energy into Sarah. I didn't have time to worry about offending anyone.

No, I needed to put all of my energy into finding the teen who'd been entrusted to my care.

"I'm going to go talk to some more of Sarah's friends," Chase said an hour later as he headed toward the school exit.

I followed on his heels. "I'm going with you."

"That's not a good idea, Holly."

"Of course it is."

Chase stopped and turned toward me, that familiar, stern look in his eyes. "Holly, let me do my job."

"I am. I'm just going to help you."

"Holly . . ." The warning in his voice turned into compassion.

I faced him, feeling some déjà vu. We'd had many conversations about things like this before. Or maybe *arguments* would be a better word.

"You know I'm just going to do this on my own," I said. "Right behind you. And is there any update on the license plate?"

He frowned and glanced down the hall behind me. "The car was stolen last week. I have another detective going to talk to the owner again, just in case there are any leads there."

I said nothing, just waited for Chase to agree to let me come. After a moment, he sighed and nodded. "Don't make me regret it."

"I won't. Besides, you know Sarah's friends will talk to me over you. It's just a fact. Most of these kids don't like cops."

"I can't argue with that." He waved his hand in the air. "Come on."

I scrambled behind him and climbed into his neat and clean unmarked police car. I could smell hints of his woodsy aftershave and the aroma of the apple-scented air freshener plugged into the charger.

I'd bought Chase one after he'd told me about just how horrid some criminals he arrested smelled. Many were drunk, had urinated on themselves, and were dirty, sweaty, and a plethora of other things that made their stench unbearable.

I was glad to see he'd kept up with the air freshener. Even better, it was made with essential oils so it wasn't rotting his lungs with every breath.

For a split second, it felt like old times. My heart twisted with bittersweet memories of when I'd felt like I was walking on the clouds with Chase by my side. Then I remembered the problems between us.

It might take two people to cause problems in a relationship, but Chase was the only one who could resolve his issues.

"How are you, Holly?" he asked as he cranked the engine. His voice sounded low. Quiet. Serious.

I bobbed my head up and down, trying to think of something interesting but honest to say. There was nothing. My life had been a routine of working, fostering, and dating Drew—as well as volunteering whenever I could. I'd seriously cut back my hours since I took up fostering.

"I can't complain," I finally said, figuring that was a safe enough response. "You?"

Chase programmed an address into his GPS, and we started down the road. "I've been working a lot."

More like burying himself in his work, I figured. I knew how that went. If I let it, my career would consume me also. But life was too short for that.

"I'm sure your job keeps you very busy," I said, reminding myself that it wasn't my business to make sure he was taking care of himself. Not anymore.

"Are you still working for your brother?"

"Yes, I am," I said. "It definitely has its challenges, but I'm glad I can help Ralph out."

"And your family? How are they?"

"They're doing fine. My mom is Ms. Community Mover and heading up more fundraisers than I can keep track of—on top of selling houses, of course. My sister loves being a mom."

"And I bet you're loving being an aunt."

I smiled as I remembered Karalena, my three-month-old niece. "I am."

I started to ask Chase if there were any updates on his brother's death but stopped. That would be insensitive. And nosy. And none of my business anymore.

His brother, Hayden, had been killed, and the murderer had never been found. It was one of the reasons Chase gave for not committing. He needed answers first.

But those answers might not ever come. Ever. Not in this life.

It was just as well. Maybe Chase was just using that as an excuse not to commit.

We pulled up to a tall, skinny house with bright purple siding. One of Sarah's friends lived here. Allison. I didn't have the girl's phone number, so she wasn't one of the people I'd called earlier.

I hoped—and prayed—that we'd find some answers.

CHAPTER 4

TEN MINUTES LATER, we were seated in a messy living room full of scattered toys, laundry waiting to be folded, and leftover afterschool snacks. Allison Ripley sat across from Chase and me, and her parents stood behind her.

I'd met Allison a few times before. She was a quiet girl whose hair matched the color of her house. She wore oversized glasses so large that they rubbed against her cheeks, and dark clothing that looked too small.

Her parents seemed normal. Her dad wore a mechanic's uniform and looked like he'd just gotten home from work. Her mom was slightly overweight, with bobbed brown hair and a baby on her hip. The sounds of kids playing—or was it fighting?—upstairs echoed through the ceiling, punctuated with an occasional loud stomping or banging above us.

Since Sarah had remained at the same school when she came to live with me, that meant she'd kept her old friends there. Originally, I'd assumed that was a good thing and that Sarah needed some stability. Now I wondered if that was true at all. Had I allowed parts of her past to keep a stronghold in her life? Bad parts? Parts I didn't know about?

Before Chase could start the conversation, I did. I locked gazes with Allison and snapped into social worker mode. "Allison, we need your help."

Allison's eyes widened. She was obviously scared and nervous and kept glancing anxiously at Chase, like this might be some kind of trap. "What's going on?"

"Do you know where Sarah went after school today?" I asked.

Allison shrugged and drew in a tight breath. "She went home, I assumed."

"She didn't mention anything else?" I asked. "Maybe a secret project or something? She won't be in trouble. I just need to know Sarah is okay. That's the important thing. I'm worried about her."

"She didn't mention anything to me." Allison rubbed her hands on her ripped jeans. "Is she okay?"

"Most likely," I answered. "But we'd like to know for sure. Is there anything you know that might be able to help us?"

"Even if it seems insignificant, it could prove useful," Chase added.

Allison shook her head a little too rapidly. "I . . . I don't know. She liked living with you, Ms. Holly. She said you were nice."

"I liked having her live with me also. I'd like for her to stay living with me for as long as possible." I'd even wondered if I could adopt Sarah. Part of me thought the idea was outrageous and the other part felt certain I should go for it.

"She talked about her real mom some," Allison said. "I think Sarah was curious about why her mom left her."

Chase straightened. "Did she go looking for her?"

"I don't think so. I mean, Sarah wouldn't have had time. She went to school, came home, did her homework, and had dinner with you, Ms. Holly. It wasn't like she had the chance to hop on the computer and search. She told me you wouldn't let her use social media. She really didn't like that."

"People are too irresponsible with it," I muttered, not wanting to get into a debate about this now. People's opinions on the issue were too strong. "Is there anything else?"

Allison shook her head again, frowning with apology. "I'm sorry. I wish I could remember something."

I tried to hold back my disappointment. But with

every minute that passed with Sarah still gone, I knew the chances of finding her decreased.

I'd hoped this was a misunderstanding. That she'd gone home with a friend. That there was some kind of excuse I could swallow until Sarah returned.

But now I wasn't so sure that was true.

Chase and I were both quiet as we climbed back into his car. We both seemed to be processing, and silence surrounded us, if only for a few seconds, after we left Allison's.

"You mind if I look at Sarah's things?" Chase asked. "Her room, in particular?"

"Of course you can," I said. "Whatever helps find her."

He started toward my house, not needing directions. We didn't even need words or platitudes. No, we'd both been around the block before, and we knew how this might turn out. Besides, I'd prefer that Chase not try to give me false hope. *Hope deferred makes the heart sick, but a longing fulfilled is a tree of life. Proverbs 13:12.*

As soon as we stepped inside my house, I was again swept back in time. I'd had hopes of Chase helping me with the improvements here. Of him being the manpower behind my decorating ideas.

I'd hoped we would dance on this wooden floor and share kisses on the couch, and I'd wondered if one day we might both live here—as husband and wife.

I tried to ignore the emptiness that echoed inside me at the memories.

I had Drew now. Why did I keep forgetting that? Drew, who treated me like a princess. Who was refined and gorgeous and mature.

He was everything on my list of the Perfect Husband.

I hadn't expected seeing Chase to stir up all these old feelings.

And I didn't like it.

"Where's Sarah's room?" Chase asked, turning toward me. Did he feel the tension too? Was he reliving memories? Or had he put us behind him and moved on?

I didn't know.

I snapped back to the moment. "Follow me."

I led him down the hallway to the bedroom across from my own. I opened the door and moved out of the way to let Chase do his job. As he began searching, I leaned against the wall, hating the hollowness inside me. Hating not knowing.

Part of me hoped that at any minute, I'd hear Sarah at the door, coming in with some explanation about what had happened. My gut told me that was unlikely, but the optimist in me tried to prevail.

From the nightstand beside her bed, I picked up a

picture of Sarah that I'd taken at a café downtown. We'd gone there on a Saturday, two weeks after she first arrived at my place. Sarah had told me it was the first fancy meal she'd ever had. The thing was, it wasn't even that fancy.

But it had been a nice day, and we'd sat outside on the bustling city sidewalk under a dark green awning. She'd ordered a salad with a fancy-looking iced tea infused with ginger and apple, and she'd told me about herself. It really had been a turning point for the two of us, a moment where I'd felt the first hope that the girl might actually trust me one day.

That feeling of hope had only continued to grow until Sarah eventually opened up to me some. I really thought we'd come a long way since she'd first come into my home with that distant, detached look in her eyes.

Which made this even harder.

Chase reached into the desk and held up a scrap of paper. "You recognize this phone number?"

I squinted as I stared at the digits, praying that something would click in place in my mind. But it didn't. "I have no idea."

"I found it stuffed between the pages of a novel in this drawer. I'll give it a call, just in case it's significant."

"We should explore every possibility."

"How about this? You recognize this woman?" Chase reached between the pages of the same book and pulled out a picture this time.

I took the photo from Chase and stared at it. The snapshot looked like a fairly recent picture of Sarah standing with a woman in her thirties. Was that Sarah's mom? It could be. The woman was Hispanic with the same dark hair that Sarah sported.

I squinted. And maybe—just maybe—they did share the same thin nose and thick eyebrows.

"I'm not sure," I finally said. "It could be her mom . . . But I didn't think the two of them had spoken in years. I really have no idea."

"I'll see if I can find out."

Just then, another thought hit me. How could I not have remembered this earlier? I rushed into my kitchen and opened the fridge.

All her insulin was there.

I rushed toward a drawer and jerked it open. I counted the items inside, just to be sure.

All of Sarah's diabetes supplies were here. The insulin injectors. The infusion set. The test strips. Nothing was missing. No, we still had an eight-day supply left.

Which meant that Sarah would be needing a new dose of insulin soon. Very soon, lest she go into diabetic ketoacidosis, a potentially life-threatening condition.

33

CHAPTER 5

AN HOUR LATER, I was at my mom's place for an emergency family meeting. Normally, I would have baked something for an event like this—cookies, cakes, and brownies almost always put people at ease—but I'd had no time today. I hadn't stopped since Sarah disappeared—and I didn't see myself stopping until I found her.

Something about being at my childhood home always filled me with comfort. The quaint house, one that smelled like orange, rosemary, and vanilla, reminded me of my dad, who'd created so many of the personal touches here. He'd been a woodworker, and he'd added nooks and crannies and even a hidden doorway leading to the library.

I'd had a great childhood, but my life looked different

now. My dad had passed away, and my mom was dating again. I wasn't a little girl struggling to fit in with my older brother and sister, who were type A, success-driven individuals. I'd been the idealist who'd go poor if it meant doing something I believed in. Sometimes, those previous chapters of my life seemed so long ago, and other times they felt like just yesterday.

I glanced around the *Better Homes and Gardens*-worthy living room. My mom and her boyfriend, Larry Truman, were here, as were the rest of my family.

My sister, Alex, her husband, William, and Karalena.

Ralph.

My best friend, Jamie, with her boyfriend, Wesley.

Drew stood beside me, offering his everlasting help.

I felt incredibly fortunate to have such a great support system. Sure, we all drove each other crazy sometimes. But when it was important, we were there for each other. And that was what mattered.

"So, here's what we know," I started.

I gave them a rundown on Sarah's disappearance, starting from the top and ending with what Chase had found in her bedroom. I'd actually called Chase "the detective assigned to the case." No need to stir up speculation. Nope, everyone needed to put their drama energy into finding Sarah instead of speculating about my love life.

Just as I finished, the doorbell rang. My mom went to

answer and returned a moment later with a smile on her face. "Holly, it's for you."

For me? But my circle was here.

I excused myself and walked toward the front entrance. I sucked in a breath when I saw Chase standing there, lines of exhaustion on his face. I wanted to offer him some coffee and a warm meal. When was the last time he'd slept? And I wasn't talking about this case—I'd bet he'd been going nonstop for months.

I swallowed the lump in my throat. "Long time, no see."

He nodded toward me. "Holly. I figured I'd find you here. And then I saw your Mustang parked outside and knew."

"Is everything okay?" The only reason Chase would show up was if something was wrong.

"I thought I'd let you know that we've found the car Sarah got into after school today."

I sucked in a breath as everything went still around me. "And?"

"There were no indicators inside of what happened, but we're searching for DNA evidence now."

My stomach clenched tighter. "Any signs of struggle?"

"No."

"Was there a GPS locater in it to show you where the car has been?"

"The vehicle was too old."

I started to ask him about the phone number and the photo, but Drew stepped into the room. He quickly assessed Chase and offered a curt nod. Then he stepped toward me and put his arm around my waist.

Was he showing that I was his? Being territorial?

Or was I reading too much into this? I didn't know.

"Everything okay?" Drew murmured.

I shook my head, still trying to process Chase's words. "They found the car Sarah got into but not Sarah."

Drew pulled his lips together in a grim line. "She probably ran away, Holly."

I shook my head again. "No, she wouldn't do that."

"It makes the most sense. It's not like she was forced into the car at gunpoint. You said you saw the video yourself."

Why was he bringing this up now? "There's more to this story. Sarah was adjusting to life with me. She had nothing to run away from."

"Didn't you say you just had a fight with her a couple nights ago?" Drew reminded me.

The muscles around my spine clenched. "We had a conversation where I had to set boundaries. It was uncomfortable but hardly a fight."

If I could shoot daggers with my eyes, that was what I'd be doing at Drew right now. Just because Sarah and I had discussed the perils of social media and because I'd told her she couldn't have a cell phone yet didn't mean we'd fought. I'd simply set boundaries.

"I'm not giving up." My voice sounded close to a growl.

Drew's hand moved to my shoulder, and he gently massaged it. "I'm not suggesting you do."

"Holly, can I have a word alone with you?" Chase's gaze slid from Drew's hand on my shoulder to my eyes.

Drew stiffened beside me, but I ignored it. He was a big boy, and certainly he understood that some situations required privacy. At least, I hoped he did.

"Of course."

Chase and I walked together into the library. My eyes closed for only a second as I remembered being a high schooler and playing Louis Armstrong and dreaming about Chase in the comfy chair in the corner. Even back then, I'd liked him—back when I'd been a dorky band nerd and he'd been the homecoming king.

"I looked into that phone number we found," he started. "It goes to a burner phone."

"Aren't burner phones only used by criminals?"

"Contrary to what's portrayed on TV, a lot of people use burner phones. Not having a contract has its appeal to people who are on a tight budget."

"I can see that. But still, I don't like this." I'd been *so* hoping for a lead, for good news.

"I also contacted the social worker about that photo. We think the picture is of Sarah's bio mom."

I sucked in a deep breath. "What sense does that make? Sarah hasn't talked to her since she was seven."

"As far as you know," Chase added.

I hated to admit he was right, but he was right. "True."

"We were able to get into Sarah's locker, but we didn't find anything. We also followed up on Sarah's bio dad, but he's still in prison. No one has been to see him in months, so we don't believe he has anything to do with this."

"Good to know."

"Lastly, we put the word out at local hospitals and clinics, in case someone brings Sarah in because of her medical condition."

"Could we do an AMBER Alert or something, Chase? Maybe start a social media campaign? I just feel like there's something more."

"AMBER Alerts are tricky, and, in this situation, I don't think it would get approved. As far as taking it to social media . . . that's between you and Family Services. You know how they are about putting these kids' names and faces online. There are a lot of privacy issues. And if they think Sarah ran away on her own . . ."

I frowned. He was right. I knew he was. But it didn't seem fair.

"I just wanted to give you an update because I know you're feeling anxious."

Unfortunately, this update only made me feel more anxious. "That's it? Nothing else?"

"No, not yet. I promise you we're working on this."

"Do you think she ran away, like Drew thinks?" I desperately wanted Chase to be on my side. I couldn't let myself believe that Sarah had left of her own accord. But what if I needed a reality check?

"Based on what you've told me, no, I don't. But we don't have any good, solid leads yet, Holly. If you hear from her, you'll let me know?"

"Absolutely."

"Thanks."

We stared at each other another moment. I could sense there were unsaid things that needed to be said. But I didn't know what they were. And I wasn't even sure we should go there.

So I stayed silent.

Finally, Chase nodded toward the door. "I should go."

I wanted to ask why he'd felt the need to tell me this in person. He could have easily called. But I didn't bring it up. No, I didn't thrive on awkward conversations.

As we stepped out the door and rounded the corner back toward the foyer, my family appeared.

And when they appeared, they *really* appeared.

It was like a long, lost son had returned home. Hugs

went around. Lots of chitchat. Chase held my niece, the baby looking even smaller against his giant frame.

I glanced at Drew during the reunion and saw him standing back, hands in his pockets, soaking the entire scene in. And he didn't look happy about it. Not in a rude way, but in an analytical, introverted way.

My heart panged with regret.

Why were relationships so sticky? So complicated? But the choices we made yesterday affected our todays. And they affected our futures.

The same could be said for Sarah. Her past had made her into the person she was today. My question was: What had happened in her past that led to the crisis today? And would I ever be able to discover it in time?

Drew insisted on following me home. It was sweet, really. We hadn't had a chance to talk since Chase had shown up at my mom's, and I could sense he had something on his mind.

As soon as my front door shut, and we were alone, my theory was proven true.

Drew turned toward me and gently asked, "Why do you act different when Chase comes around?"

I shrugged, feeling like the walls were closing in on

me, and there was no good reason for it other than my own anxieties. "Because he's my ex. It's always weird being around your ex."

Drew stared deeply into my eyes. "Not because you have feelings for him?"

"Feelings for him?" I nearly snorted, which was so unladylike. "No. I'm not acting weird around him because I have feelings for him."

I chose my words carefully. I didn't want to be deceitful. But the truth was I *might* have feelings for Chase. But feelings didn't matter. What mattered were decisions. And Drew was the one I was dating. I wouldn't let my emotions dictate my actions. That only ended in disaster

Drew rubbed my arms. "Good. I'm glad to hear that. I was getting a little nervous."

"Don't be nervous."

His arms slid around me, and he pulled me into a hug. "I'm sorry about all of this, Holly. I know you really care for Sarah. I hope we're able to find her."

I could hear the sincerity in his voice. Drew liked Sarah and had been good to her. Her disappearance wasn't just hard on me, but it affected him also.

"Me too," I finally said. "I don't think I'll get any rest until I know she's okay. I just can't imagine what happened to her."

"Why would anyone abduct her?"

I shrugged, annoyed by his question even though I shouldn't be. "I don't know. Why does anyone ever abduct anyone? People have some pretty twisted motives."

"I'm just saying. She doesn't have money. Her parents aren't in her life. So why?"

"I don't even want to think about it. But there are horrible reasons. Believe me."

"Oh, I know." He hugged me tighter. "I wish I could do something."

"Thanks for being here for me. That means a lot." Drew was selfless. A hard worker. A man of faith.

There was nothing not to like about him—except when he occasionally inserted himself into my investigative nosiness.

"Speaking of that," he glanced at his watch, "I have to run to the funeral home. Do you want me to see if someone else can take this call?"

I shook my head. "No, of course not. Go ahead. I'll be fine."

Some space by myself actually sounded good. I needed to think. To snoop. And I couldn't do that right now with Drew giving me all his undying attention.

He planted a soft kiss on my cheek. "Okay, I'll call you later. Sound good?"

"Sounds great."

As soon as the door closed, I turned back and faced my house. I knew Chase had checked things out earlier, that he'd looked for evidence about what had happened to Sarah. But I was going to check again. Because a girl never knew what she might find.

CHAPTER 6

AS EXHAUSTION HIT ME, I sat on the edge of Sarah's bed.

I remembered just last night sitting here, only Sarah had been under the covers before turning in for the evening. We'd had a heart to heart about cliques at school and mean girls. I'd been trying to offer some wisdom on the situation.

"You be you, and let them be them," I'd said. "And then if while you're being you and they're being them, the two of you can be friends being friends, then so be it. But never change you to fit them."

Sarah had stared at me, looking confounded. "What?"

"I know it sounds confusing, but just give it a few minutes to sink in. It will make sense one day."

I smiled at the memory, but the grin faded.

Whose number was that you were calling, Wonder Girl? Were you looking for your mother? Were you in touch with her? Or is this about something else completely?

I didn't believe today's encounter was random. No, I'd seen Sarah smiling at the person in that car. She was familiar to her.

Nor did I think she'd run away. What I did think was that she could have been duped.

Sitting here probably wasn't helping anything. But I was at a loss as to what else I could do.

I'd been through all the training—to be a foster mom. I'd gone to parenting classes at church. Before taking Sarah into my home, I'd had to take a two-day workshop on caring for people with Type 1 diabetes.

Sarah had problems finding foster homes because of her condition. It wasn't for the faint of heart. In fact, I'd only been taking on foster kids in a respite situation—for short-term emergencies. But when Kathy had come to me about Sarah—how she desperately needed somewhere to stay—I'd prayed about it and said yes.

Erin, her previous foster mom, couldn't handle the pressure of taking care of someone with diabetes anymore. No, her husband had a heart attack, and taking care of him in the aftermath of it had become a full-time job.

My cell phone rang just then. I looked at the screen and didn't recognize the number, though the area code indicated it was local.

I put the phone to my ear and answered. "Hello?"

I waited for a response but heard nothing. Well, not *nothing* nothing. There was some kind of movement or wind that let me know someone was there, but no one spoke.

"Hello?" I said again.

Maybe someone had butt dialed me. I wasn't sure.

I started to hit End when I heard people murmuring in the background. I paused, trying to make out what was being said. But I couldn't.

I pulled the phone away from my ear and frowned. What was this about? And whose number was this?

Before I could say anything else, the line went silent. I stared at the phone a moment before dialing the number again.

It was busy. Of course.

Could the call have been from Sarah?

I didn't know. But I really hoped it wasn't a silent cry for help.

At 8:30, I decided to go to the youth center where I

volunteered. It would be open for another thirty minutes, and that was all the time I would need.

I hoped.

I went there once a week or so, and Sarah had been coming with me. She'd seemed to bond with one particular girl there, Tanya Rodgers. I wanted to see if Tanya was at the center tonight.

Ten minutes later I pulled up to a brick building located in a string of aged storefronts that used to be bustling with life. Now the area was rundown and crime-ridden, a skeleton of what it had once been.

When I got there, I found all the guys out back playing basketball. Half the girls were inside doing their nails or baking, and the other half were outside watching the boys.

Except for one.

Tanya wasn't going to let basketball be an all-guy sport. Nope, she liked to play, and no one and nothing—especially gender—was going to stop her. The girl was five foot nine inches, with dark curly hair and tanned skin.

I stood on the sidelines for a minute until there was a break in the game. And then I called her over.

She threw the ball to Antonio and walked toward me. "What's going on, Ms. Holly? Where's Sarah?"

"That's what I was hoping to talk to you about. Could I have a minute?"

"Yeah, sure." She followed me over to a corner beside the chain-link fence, sweat pouring down her cheeks and forehead.

The girl was athletic, and I kept encouraging her to continue working on long-distance running. Seriously, if the girl had money, she would be an Olympic-level athlete by now. Well, money, a great coach, a supportive community, and the drive to do it.

"Sarah disappeared after school today," I started.

"What?" Tanya's eyes widened with surprise.

I nodded solemnly. "I haven't heard from her, and I'm worried. Do you have any idea where she might be?"

"No, no clue. Is Sarah okay?"

"I hope she is. That's what I'm trying to figure out, but answers have been hard to find. I know she talks to you sometimes. I was hoping you might have an idea . . ."

Tanya's gaze shifted from shock to realization before she looked down, as if trying to cover up what her eyes revealed.

"Anything you know might help, Tanya."

She shrugged unconvincingly. "I don't know anything."

"Please, Tanya. I can see it in your eyes. You know something. What if Sarah is in danger?"

She glanced up. Looked into the distance. Her jaw muscles flexed. Her shoulders straightened.

"Sarah met a guy," she finally muttered.

My heart rate spiked. "A guy?"

Tanya nodded stiffly. "Online, but I know she wanted to meet him in real life too."

"Tell me more."

A sigh escaped, and Tanya glanced around. "Like I said, Sarah met him online, and she wanted to meet him in person. Maybe I shouldn't be telling you all of this stuff . . ."

"No, please. I need to know. Go ahead." I prayed she would keep talking. I needed answers.

Tanya's jaw jumped, but she finally said, "They met on Chatbook."

"But Sarah doesn't have a Chatbook page."

Tanya snorted. "She does. You just don't know about it."

A sick feeling gurgled in my gut. Had I been that clueless? "Okay. Did she use an alias or something?"

"Sarah Rae. She's had the page for forever—for as long as I've known her, at least. She met the guy there. He sounded perfect, she said. Athletic. From a good family. He never made her feel bad or like she was less important since she was in the foster system."

The guy could be a winner . . . or a predator. I really hoped he wasn't a predator, but I also knew the odds. They weren't good. "Go on."

"They've been talking for a month or so."

She'd been with me for two months. How had I not known this? "And?"

Tanya glanced around again. No kid in this area wanted to be a tattletale. But this was important, and Tanya had to know that.

"He wanted to meet. Last time I talked to Sarah, she didn't know when or where. But if she's gone, my guess is that she's with him."

"You've been a big help, Tanya. Thank you."

"Ms. Holly?" Her face twisted with distress.

"Yes?"

"Sarah told me one time that the hardest part about being in the foster system was the fact that she could disappear and no one would ever notice."

My heart felt like it stopped as I processed her words. No one should ever feel like that. No one.

Hearing her words only made my resolve strengthen. "I noticed, and I'm not going to make that a reality for her."

"I'm glad." Tanya lowered her voice. "Don't tell anyone here I told you, okay?"

"It's a deal."

I stared at my phone. Who should I call? Drew? He was working with a family on burial arrangements. And crime solving wasn't really his thing.

Chase? This was definitely his thing. He needed to know. It was his job.

Guilt plagued me a minute as my loyalties battled it out.

Then I called Chase.

CHAPTER 7

"I'M NOT HER FRIEND, so I can't see any of her posts." I leaned back in the desk chair and suppressed a sigh, choosing instead to run a hand over my face to try and wipe away the tension.

Chase sat beside me in a kitchen chair that we'd pulled up to Sarah's desk in her room. I'd brought my laptop in here, hoping to get into Sarah's headspace in the process. So far, it hadn't worked.

"We have guys who can get around this." Chase turned in the chair to face me. "I don't suppose you know Sarah's user name or password?"

"I didn't even know she had an account."

"This is fairly typical, Holly." Compassion stretched across his voice.

"I've never wanted to be fairly typical." I heard the

irritation in my tone and cringed. I didn't want to be so nasty, but I was tired and stressed and worried. Manners were the last thing on my mind right now.

"No, you never have, have you? But this isn't just a problem with kids in the foster care system. This is becoming an increasing problem with teens across the country. Social media and technology have taken over their lives, and many of them don't have enough good sense or experience to know where to draw lines."

"Life was better when people connected in person, don't you think?"

"I do." Chase smiled, a nostalgic look in his eyes. "It's good to talk to you again, Holly. I always appreciate your perspective. It's refreshing."

"It's good to talk to you again too. How are you doing? How are you *really* doing, Chase?" I'd asked earlier, but the conversation had been superficial. Maybe I needed to change the conversation for a minute in order to clear my thoughts, allowing room for some fresh thinking later. Because banging my head against an imaginary wall was getting me nowhere.

"I'm hanging in."

Are you dating anyone? Any updates on your brother? You haven't reverted back to drinking, have you?

I kept those questions silent, but that was what I really wanted to know. I wanted a heart-to-heart—which would be a terrible idea. Wisdom told me I should keep my distance.

"Karalena sure is a beauty," Chase said.

"Isn't she, though? My sister just seems so happy." Alex was basically living the life I'd envisioned myself living. I tried not to be jealous.

Chase let out a long sigh, one that seemed to be fraught with memories of better times. I understood.

His phone rang. He put it to his ear and stepped toward the corner of the room. I tried to listen in, but my phone rang also.

I glanced at the screen. It was Drew. My heart rate kicked up a notch.

I answered and stepped into the hallway. "Hey."

"Hey, sweetie. Any updates?"

"No, nothing yet. Not really. Only leads that aren't leading anywhere."

"I'm sorry to hear that. I've been praying for answers."

"Thank you. We need all the prayers we can get. I guess you're back from the funeral home."

"I am. It was a long day."

"I'm sorry." I leaned against the wall, exhausted but fighting it.

"No, I'm sorry. My bad day doesn't compare to yours." He paused. "Is that someone talking in the background?"

I sucked in a breath and looked over my shoulder. Chase was on the phone in Sarah's room.

I hadn't realized his voice would carry this far.

Say it's the TV.

I closed my eyes. The thought was so tempting. But I couldn't lie. *Integrity is who you are when no one is looking.* My dad had always said that.

"It's . . . it's actually Chase."

"Chase?" Drew's voice went rigid. "What's he doing with you?"

"I thought I had a new lead, so I called him."

A beat passed. "Instead of me?"

I clenched my eyes shut tighter. "He *is* the detective on the case, and you were working."

Another pause. "Is he at your house, Holly?"

Guilt plagued me. "He is, but in a professional manner. This is nothing to get upset about."

"You're my girlfriend. I trust you. But . . ."

I moved farther from Chase, too exhausted to distinguish whether my guilt was justified or not. "But what?"

Drew let out a sigh. "I don't know, Holly. I'm sorry. I just . . . it's just weird for me."

I nibbled on my bottom lip, thankful for his honesty and his attempt at understanding. "I'm not trying to make things weird. I'm just trying to find Sarah."

"I know that. And I want you to find her. I just don't want you running back into your ex's arms."

I glanced at Chase. "I'm not going to do that, Drew. I didn't take you as a jealous type."

"I'm not. But I am realistic."

"Drew . . ." How did I even begin to explain my thoughts? And was the fact that I missed Chase and that I mourned the loss of our relationship a sign that I shouldn't be with Drew? Was I floundering in unsafe relationship territory without realizing it? I had high standards for myself, and I wanted to do the right thing. Think the right things. Dwell on the right things.

So why did I feel so confused?

"Look, forget about it. We can talk later. I just wanted an update."

My heart twisted into knots inside my chest. This was the last thing I wanted or needed right now.

"Okay. Goodnight, Drew."

"Goodnight, Holly."

"Everything okay?" Chase asked as I walked back inside of Sarah's bedroom.

Unfortunately, after dating for so long, he could read me like a book. "I'm fine."

"You look pale."

"It's nothing concerning this case. Just . . . something personal."

"Understood." He turned back to the computer, his fingers poised at the keyboard. "Any guesses what Sarah's

59

password or user name might be, now that you've had time to think about it?"

I sighed, hating the fact that I'd been deceived and hating that I'd been so trusting. Foster mom fail #103. "What do we get? Three strikes and we're out?"

"Usually."

That meant I needed some good ideas.

I opened Sarah's desk drawer and riffled through some of her papers. It was mostly schoolwork. A few drawings. Nothing that seemed overly important.

I paused when I got to her planner. Sarah had told me she liked to do things the old school way and write down due dates for assignments in an old notebook. I'd introduced her to the idea of using a calendar/planner instead, and she'd begun organizing her school schedule that way.

I flipped through the pages there, and at the end I paused.

"Chase, what is this?" I pointed to a notation written on the last page where a person could record their height and weight.

Lonergirl357

239Forever

"It looks like a user name and password to me," Chase said.

"I know Sarah would always say she had a hard time remembering things."

"Let's give it a shot."

He typed it into the log-in page. A moment later, the screen changed.

It had worked.

We were on.

Now I hoped we could find out something.

CHAPTER 8

"LOOK AT THAT! He must be the guy Sarah has been talking to." Excitement—and worry—tinged my voice as I stared at the thumbnail-sized photo of the guy who'd befriended Sarah. "Can you click on his profile?"

"Of course."

A moment later, the guy's page came up. His name was Cameron Lane. According to what I read, he was a college student at University of Cincinnati. In his photos, he had thick dark hair, a big smile, and an affinity for selfies—which should always be the first sign not to date someone.

"A college guy? Did he know Sarah was only fourteen?" My stomach turned as the question left my lips. Situations like these rarely turned out well.

"You don't really want me to tell you about some of the things I've seen online," Chase said.

"No, I don't. But I know there are predators out there who prey on younger girls."

"Especially girls who don't have a strong family system."

"She had me." My voice sounded a bit pathetic, but Chase's words had stung, even though I knew they shouldn't.

"These kids . . . their brains are wired a different way, Holly." His voice sounded low and cautious.

"I know. But I still have hope that I can break through and reach them. Does that make me crazy?"

"No, it makes you a blessing to them."

My cheeks warmed at Chase's compliment. I cleared my throat, pulling myself out of my self-pity. This wasn't about me. It was about Sarah, and I'd be wise to keep that in mind. "Can we pull up their message history?"

Chase hit a few more keys, and the screen changed from mostly pictures to mostly text. "Here it is."

I leaned closer and read the messages. Their first correspondence was dated one month ago, just like Tanya had indicated.

The chat originally started when Cameron contacted Sarah and said he'd noticed after a search on the site that she had diabetes. He was thinking about getting an insulin pump and wanted to know what she thought of it.

"Smooth line," I muttered.

"You'd be surprised how many of these people strike up conversations like this," Chase said. "They find something in common and exploit it."

From there, the two of them chatted about diabetes and what it was like to live with the disease. Sarah never told Cameron her age. Nor did she ever mention her age on her profile. Was that on purpose? If I had to guess, I'd say yes.

Truthfully, the girl in the pictures looked closer to eighteen than fourteen. I supposed most girls thought that was more flattering—to appear older. At least when you were a teenager.

I just wished teens would enjoy their youth while they could. It was over way too quickly.

Finally, we got to the end of the messages. I drew in a deep breath.

They'd talked about meeting. Today.

"This has to be our guy, Chase," I said.

"I agree."

I straightened. "Let's go find him."

And maybe find Sarah too.

"Holly, we can't leave right now. It's 2:00 a.m."

Time didn't matter right now. "But what if he has Sarah?"

Chase shook his head. "We need a search warrant. We

need more evidence. You did a great job here. Now I need to take over and do this the right way."

"But—"

Chase stood, his mind obviously made up and his voice leaving no room for argument. "Holly, you've got to promise me you won't go find this guy on your own."

Yet I couldn't stop myself from arguing. "But—"

"There aren't any buts. I need you to promise, Holly. If you approach him in the wrong way, he could hide Sarah away, and we'd never find her."

Well, since he said it like that . . .

The snarky thought was immediately followed by a burst of anxiety. What if we never found Sarah? If we never got any answers? No, I couldn't think like that.

Finally, I nodded. "I promise. But, if there's any way possible, could I go with you? I mean, just in case you find Sarah. I want to be there. She'll be scared."

He hesitated before nodding. "I'll see what I can do. You just wait."

Chase knew me too well. Knew I was horrible at waiting.

But, for Sarah's sake, I was going to have to do just that and pray for the best in the meantime.

My phone rang again. It was the same number that had called earlier.

I quickly answered, expecting to hear nothing again.

Instead, I heard those voices in the background.

Except this time, I could barely make out what was being said.

It was a whisper really, a whisper that stretched slightly louder than the background noise.

And the caller said, "Holly, please help me. Please."

"Sarah? Sarah? Is that you?" My voice trembled as I said the words.

Chase appeared beside me and indicated for me to put the phone on speaker. My hands trembled, but I did as he said.

I heard the voices in the background, but nothing else. No more whispers.

"Sarah, are you there? It's me. Can you hear me?"

Still nothing.

I glanced at Chase and saw the concern on his face as well. He motioned for me to keep talking.

"We're looking for you, Sarah," I said, my voice a quivering mess. "Can you give me a hint about where you are?"

Nothing again.

I listened to the voices in the background. I didn't hear any distress—no yelling or screaming. Was it a party?

I just had no idea.

Before I could ask anything else, the phone went silent. I held my breath, waiting to see what happened.

But the screen went blank, and I realized the call had been cut off.

"Tell me what she said," Chase said.

"She said, 'Holly, help me. Please.'" My heart panged as I said the words.

"Was it Sarah?"

"I can't say with 100 percent certainty, but my gut tells me yes. Who else would it be?"

"Could you make out anything else being said in the background?"

"No, I tried. But it just sounded like people talking." My eyes met Chase's. "What do you think this means?"

"I don't know, Holly. But I don't like this."

CHAPTER 9

I WAITED until six that morning before I called Chase for an update.

I thought I was being pretty generous, especially considering I'd been up all night, waiting to hear from him.

I'd already showered—I took my phone with me in a plastic bag in case Chase or Sarah called—and afterward I had gotten dressed. I downed an entire pot of coffee, and now I felt jittery.

I'd also made some sugar-free blueberry muffins, just because that was what I did when I got stressed, and they were Sarah's favorites. If we found her and she came home today, I wanted to have them waiting for her.

When Chase answered, he sounded like he'd been up all night also.

"I'm sorry to bug you, Chase," I started, pacing in my living room and wishing I hadn't had so much caffeine. I felt it coursing through my body and heard it coursing through my voice as well. "I really am. But I can't sleep. And . . ."

"We literally just got the warrant, and I'm about to head out to talk to Cameron. Would you like to join me?"

"Yes!" Relief burst through me. I could go! I couldn't express how happy I was to hear that. I hated being left out in the cold, and my former position as a social worker, as well as my current position as a community liaison for a state senator, did afford me a few privileges.

"You can't play an active part in this, Holly."

"I know."

His voice shifted from informational to concerned. "And you need to brace yourself for whatever the outcome is. If we find Sarah. If we don't find her. If we find her, and it's not the scenario you envisioned."

"I'm bracing myself. I am." I'd mentally gone over all those scenarios last night. It was part of the reason I couldn't sleep.

Still, Chase hesitated. "Okay then."

I'd tried to do a little research last night on this Cameron guy, but I hadn't been successful. Obviously, he was using an alias. I'd searched his friend list, but I hadn't recognized any names. There were no obviously controversial posts of pictures—then again, predators would be smarter than that.

All it had amounted to was a bunch of worry and no real answers.

Chase picked me up twenty minutes later. He looked as tired as I felt, and there were three empty cups of coffee in the holder between the front seats.

"Morning," I muttered, feeling for a minute that old times were upon us again.

But I couldn't slip into that way of thinking. Chase and I had moved beyond being engaged, and we were now charting the unknown waters of friendship. I'd thought about it a lot during my restless hours of unrest last night.

Just because my initial reaction to being around Chase had been a bit of mourning for the past, that didn't mean I was going to dwell in that place. No, I was moving on and had drawn mental boundaries for myself.

This whole friendship thing was going to be much harder than I anticipated. But I owed it to myself and Chase to try. Mostly, I owed it to Drew.

"So, this is the update," Chase said. "Cameron Lane is actually Cameron Penki. And he's not actually in college, but he works at a clothing store at the mall."

"Where does Cameron live?"

"With his parents."

This wasn't sounding good. "Any criminal record?"

"None. He was in his school's marching band. He likes microbreweries. He can burp the alphabet."

"Interesting." I didn't know what to think of all this, to be honest.

"Let's go see what he has to say." We pulled up to a decent, middle-class house in a neighborhood on the east side of Cincinnati. Two marked police cars pulled up behind us.

Chase turned to me before we got out of his car. "Remember, let me do the talking or you're out of this. I mean it, Holly."

I nodded obediently. "Got it."

I followed behind Chase as we walked to the front door. But my hands were shaking.

Was Sarah inside? Had this man hurt her? Or had this meet-up been a mutual thing?

I hoped Cameron had some answers.

A woman answered the door a moment later. She had her bathrobe pulled around her, and her eyes looked fresh with sleep. "Can I help you?"

She sounded annoyed. It was early, so maybe she had good reason.

"We need to speak to Cameron," Chase said.

"And you are?"

"The police." Chase held his badge in one hand and the warrant in the other. "I'm Detective Chase Dexter of the Cincinnati P.D. We have a few questions for Cameron as well as a warrant to search your place."

Before she could object, the officers flooded inside. Chase also stepped inside, probably to block the woman from closing the door on us.

Her face showed her obvious surprise and concern—as anyone's would. For a moment, I felt sorry for her. Did she have any idea what her son was up to? Most likely, no.

She gasped. "Is everything okay?"

"That's what we're hoping to find out."

"Let me get him." She scurried toward the back of the house.

I held my breath, hoping this went smoothly. Maybe I'd watched too many TV shows where the bad guys took off in a run or escaped out a window.

But, to my surprise, Cameron appeared down the hall two minutes later.

He wore some Spiderman pajamas and had obviously just gotten out of bed. Gone was the rich frat boy look he'd showcased on his social media profile. He was much shorter in real life and somehow looked skinnier too. He had acne, and he needed a haircut.

Social media could be such a pretentious place—one where it was too easy to be fake, to become someone you weren't.

"What's going on?" Cameron asked.

Chase held up a photo. "Do you know this girl?"

Cameron's eyes widened as he stared at the picture. "No, I don't know her."

"Let me revise my question. Have you seen the girl? We know you know her. Don't deny it. We have the social media to prove it."

His face went pale.

"Don't waste our time here, Cameron." Chase's voice sounded steely. "Sarah is missing, and we know you were supposed to meet with her."

Cameron's eyes widened, and, in the blink of an eye, he pushed past us and ran.

CHAPTER 10

CHASE CAUGHT Cameron before he even reached the end of the lawn.

I knew he would.

As Chase used an old football move to tackle him, Cameron's mom stood in the background with her hands over her mouth, little cries coming from her in horror as she watched everything.

Chase dragged him back over to us. Cameron's face showed distress. Despair. Panic.

"I didn't do anything!" His voice cracked with every other word. "I promise."

"Then why did you run?" Chase demanded, still gripping Cameron's arm.

"Because I know how all of this is going to look." Cameron's voice cracked more as it rose in pitch.

"Cameron, just talk to them," his mom pleaded, her fist over her mouth and wrinkles at the corners of her eyes. "You're making yourself seem guilty. That's how it looks."

"I'm innocent here." Cameron raised his hands in surrender, looking more like a twelve-year-old than a college student.

"Then start talking," Chase growled.

"Okay, okay."

Chase released Cameron but loomed over him, making it clear that one wrong move and he'd be ensnared again.

"I did meet Sarah online. I saw her profile and wanted to get to know her. It's hard meeting girls when you're shy."

"Go on," Chase said.

"I really liked her. I thought she was nice, and we were going to meet. But then she told me she was only fourteen, and I told her no way." Cameron's words came out fast and frantic.

"How did you tell her that?" Chase asked. "We saw your messages on Chatbook, and there was no mention of this conversation."

"We texted."

"On what?" I blurted, hoping my intrusion wasn't too intrusive—as in "I was going to be kicked out of ever tagging along again" intrusive. "Sarah didn't have a phone."

Cameron gave me an expression that clearly stated I must also believe the moon landing never took place. "Yes, she does have a phone. We texted all the time."

My mouth dropped open. How could I have not seen that? How? Fail #213.

Chase gave me a warning look, and I stepped back, clamping my mouth shut. The September sun beat down on us, but yesterday's rain was gone. A few neighbors paused to stare at the scene from their yards and porches, causing another burst of compassion for Cameron's mom.

"How did you find out about Sarah's real age?" Chase asked.

"I guess Sarah started feeling guilty, and she admitted it to me. I liked her and all, but I know the laws. There was no way I could meet her. No way."

"Cameron, what were you thinking?" His mother gawked at him, disappointment in her gaze.

"I told you! You should be proud. As soon as I realized she'd tricked me, I walked away. I did the right thing. It's not my fault she lied about her age."

"Are you sure you didn't meet her?" Chase pressed.

"I'm sure. You can see my text messages to her. I told her it was over."

"And she let it go?" Chase asked.

Cameron shrugged, his chin lifting a touch as his ego appeared to kick in. "Yeah, I mean, she wasn't happy. But what else could she say?"

"That's a great question." Chase's hands went to his hips. "What else did she say?"

"She begged to meet. I said no. And that was it. I haven't heard from her since then."

"I'm going to need to see those messages. And I need her phone number."

I held my breath. Chase could trace the number. Maybe we could find Sarah.

Just then, an officer stepped outside and called Chase over. He showed him a paper, and when Chase turned back to Cameron, fire lit his eyes.

"Can you explain the hotel reservation you made last night?"

Cameron's face lost all of its color. "It's not what you think."

"Then you better start explaining. Because what I think is that you're going to jail."

"You've got to believe me," Cameron rushed. "I made that reservation, but I canceled it."

Chase motioned for another one of his officers to check it out. The officer—Officer Henry, according to his shirt—pulled out his phone and scurried away.

"Tell me more."

"When I first thought I was going to meet Sarah—

before I knew she was fourteen—I made that reservation," Cameron said, sweat spreading like a deadly outbreak across his face.

"At a hotel?"

He shrugged. "I wanted somewhere private to meet her."

Sure he did.

"But I canceled the reservation. I never went there," Cameron continued.

"Where were you last night?" Chase pressed.

"I worked all day at the mall. I got off at six, and I came home. I was down in the basement playing video games all night." He turned to his mom. "Right, Mom? You saw me."

She nodded, trying a little too hard to look affirming. "He's telling the truth."

"Did you actually see him down there?" Chase asked.

Her neck muscles tensed. She opened her mouth. Shut it. Then she finally said, "Well, I saw him go down there after dinner. I didn't exactly go check on him . . ."

"Mom." Cameron hung his head in disappointment. Or was it exasperation?

"Detective Dexter." Officer Henry paused beside us.

Chase joined him, and I tried to keep one eye on Cameron and one ear on Chase's conversation. It took talent, but I was going to do my best.

"What he said checks out," the officer said. "The

79

reservation was canceled, and no one stayed in that room last night."

I didn't know if I was disappointed or grateful. We hadn't found Sarah, but at least she hadn't done something stupid with Cameron.

Still, where did this leave us?

I looked over at Cameron and swallowed hard, knowing I was supposed to be quiet. "Cameron, what was the phone number Sarah used when you texted? Do you have it memorized?"

"Yeah, of course." He spouted the digitals.

As he did, the color drained from my face.

That was the same number I'd gotten those two calls from yesterday.

Sarah had reached out to me.

And she was in trouble.

CHAPTER 11

CAMERON'S STORY CHECKED OUT. He was at work yesterday during the time Sarah disappeared, and multiple witnesses could verify it. He came home after work, and his car remained at home for the rest of the evening.

Chase was going to continue looking into Cameron, just to verify everything. He would check his phone records, check the GPS in his car, and delve into his social media accounts. But something told me Chase wouldn't find anything.

Chase was also going to trace Sarah's number—but he told me it would take some time, and he wasn't sure how much information it would yield.

That left me on my own. Chase had dropped me back

at my house. I'd called Drew and given him an update, and then I'd called my brother, Ralph.

I'd asked if I could make up some time off over the weekend. Ralph agreed. There were some perks to working for your brother, but I tried to be careful how much I asked of him. Nothing would make coworkers hate me as much as special privileges.

Still, this was Sarah. I wouldn't be able to concentrate at work today anyway.

As I stood in the middle of my living room, pondering what to do now, my phone buzzed, however, and reminded me that Sarah had an appointment in an hour with her physician.

I sucked in a breath.

That was right. With everything going on, I'd forgotten.

Should I cancel?

No, I decided. I wanted to find out more information from Sarah's doctor so I could know what to expect as far as her diabetes.

So I drove to the pediatrician's office, located twenty minutes away in the College Hill area of town. The building was older, and the inside outdated. Needless to say, this wasn't one of the fancy, nicer doctor's offices in the area.

But Dr. Greg Marks was supposed to be one of the best pediatric endocrinologists—or diabetes doctors—in the area. I checked in and then sat awkwardly in the waiting room. Everyone else had kids with them. But not me.

I wasn't sure how this all would go, but I was about to find out.

The nurse called me—called Sarah, actually—and squinted as she glanced at me. "I was hoping to consult with the doctor. It's a private matter."

"I'll have to check with Dr. Marks."

"Please do. It's important."

She left me in the hallway, disappeared around the corner, and returned a few minutes later still looking uncertain. "He said he'd see you in the office."

"Thank you."

I followed her to the back of the building. She extended her hand, indicating for me to go into a room. I stepped inside and saw the doctor there.

We'd met twice before, but I doubt Dr. Marks remembered me. He probably saw twenty or thirty patients a day, and there was nothing about Sarah and me that stood out.

That was why a surge of surprise washed over me when he said, "Ms. Paladin. Have a seat."

He knew my name, and I was pretty sure the nurse hadn't told him—that she didn't know my name herself.

Dr. Marks was in his early forties with a head full of blond hair, a square jaw, and gold-rimmed glasses. Based on my earlier experience with the man, he was smart, well-spoken, and had a good bedside manner.

"Thank you for seeing me." I clutched my purse on my lap.

He leaned back and knit his fingers together in front of him. "What's going on?"

"I know this is a bit unconventional, but Sarah is my foster daughter—"

"Yes, I remember the two of you. You seemed to have a good bond, even though you've been together for only a couple of months."

I pushed a hair behind my ear, impressed. "Good memory."

"Remembering people is important. Patients should be more than a number."

"Kudos to you for that." I shifted. "I'm here because Sarah has disappeared."

His eyes narrowed. "What do you mean?"

I explained what happened, only adding the important details.

He grunted when I finished. "Do the police have any leads?"

"I know they're working on it."

"I'm still not sure I understand why you're here."

"I'm concerned because of her diabetes. I know she's on the insulin pump, but I'm nearly certain she doesn't have enough medication with her. Needless to say, I'm worried."

"She didn't take any refills?"

"I counted them last night. She didn't. But she did fill and replace her insulin cartridge on the day she disappeared."

Dr. Marks straightened and opened Sarah's patient file, studying it for several minutes. "I'm just basing this on what you've told me and what I'm reading here. Of course, I have no way to know the fine details."

"Of course."

"Sarah could be okay for a couple days until she has to refill her cartridge again. But, and I'm sure you know this, she'll need her medication to successfully manage her diabetes. Insulin is . . . well, it's life support for people with this disease. Without insulin and proper management . . ."

"It's a death sentence," I finished.

My heart pounded in my ears. I'd known that was the truth. But hearing the doctor confirm my worst fears only further drove home how desperate this situation was.

"If there's anything I can do, please let me know," Dr. Marks said. "I'd be happy to speak to the police and tell them how dire this is. Whatever circumstances Sarah left under—voluntary or duress—her life is in danger."

As I stepped from the doctor's office and into the bright, sunny day outside, I spotted someone wearing a black hoodie—hood up—standing at my Mustang, peering into the window.

"Hey!" I yelled.

The person startled but didn't look at me. No, he—or she—took off in a run. I started after the person, but as I stepped down off the curb, my foot twisted and my shoe heel broke.

I glanced up.

The person was gone.

Just what was going on here?

CHAPTER 12

I MET JAMIE FOR LUNCH.

Talking with her always made everything better.

We convened at a restaurant called Joseph's, Jamie's favorite vegan, gluten-free utopia, where I ordered a salad that was probably delicious, but it was tasteless to me today. I had too many things on my mind. And I told Jamie about all of them.

"I am so sorry, girlfriend," Jamie said, putting another squirt of vinegar into her ice water and rattling the ice in her glass. "I've been praying and praying, hoping Sarah would come back home or that the police would find some leads. I can only imagine how difficult this must be."

Jamie was the kind of friend every girl needed. I could tell her all of my secrets, and I knew she'd keep them safe. Yet she was wise and imparted her wisdom to me. And even better, she prayed for me. I couldn't ask for anything more.

She was a reporter for a local paper, had lost a hundred pounds by sheer willpower—well, willpower and vinegar water—and she was a ray of sunshine in my life. Even her face reflected it. Her black hair sprung out in bouncy curls, her smile was bright and big, and her eyes displayed depths of fun-loving insight.

We hadn't been hanging out as much lately now that she'd been dating Wesley. They'd been together for the past seven months, and she seemed so happy.

I was happy for her.

She leaned closer, picking a mushroom off her pizza. "So I felt some tension in the room last night when I was with your family, Drew, and Chase."

I leaned back into the glittery upholstery of the booth, totally forgetting about my salad now. "Yeah, I was hoping I'd imagined all of that."

"Oh, no. No imagination required. Drew didn't love Chase being there. Chase didn't love Drew being there. Seriously, for a minute I felt like I was on a soap opera. How does Drew feel about you working with Chase?"

I shrugged, thankful when Harry Connick Jr. came on the overhead. He always made me feel better. As did the smell of freshly baked bread and hot, melting cheese. "What's there to feel? It's professional."

Jamie let her head fall to the side and gave me the "what for" look. "Really? You're not that naïve."

I let out a sigh, knowing better than to deny this too much. "Okay, it is weird. But just because he's my ex doesn't mean that Drew has anything to feel insecure about."

She leaned closer, her elbows pressed into the tabletop and her hands laced together. "You like Drew, right?"

"Of course I do. I mean, he's great. He pretty much marks everything off my list of qualities I want in a husband one day." Really, any girl would be lucky to end up with someone like Drew. He was basically the total package.

"I can totally see that. And I really do think he loves you."

My cheeks warmed at her words. "Yes, he does. He's told me."

Jamie tilted her head the other way, not letting me off the hook that easily. "But you still haven't told him that?"

"I just . . . I can't bring myself to say it."

"Why not?"

"I have to be sure."

"You're attracted to him, aren't you?"

I nodded, a little too quickly. "He's handsome. He has great hygiene. He's successful. Kind. He loves God. What's there not to be attracted to?"

Had I just said he had great hygiene? What kind of person said stuff like that? I mean, it was on my list, but . . .

Jamie's lips twisted as she continued to study my face. "There's just always been something about Chase, though, hasn't there?"

My stomach clenched and, for good measure, I stabbed my fork into an innocent piece of lettuce to drive home my next point. "Emotions are deceitful."

"You've been reading self-help books, haven't you?"

"Maybe. But that truth is also in the Bible. It says the heart is more deceitful than all else. I know it's true." And why could my friend read me so easily? I couldn't get away with anything.

She let out a long breath and leaned back. "I don't know what to tell you."

"There's nothing to say. I'm dating Drew. I wouldn't cheat on him."

One of her eyebrows rose, and Jamie crossed her arms, a picture of sassiness. "Remember that pride comes before a fall."

My mental gears jerked to a halt. "You think I'd cheat? Is that what you're saying?"

Jamie shrugged, like her words hadn't been a big deal. "No, I didn't say that. I'm just warning you to be careful. Chase sometimes causes you to use bad judgment."

"What? Like when?"

Her eyebrow arched higher. "Like when you practically stalked him down in Louisville."

Oh, *that*. "I wasn't stalking. I was worried about him. And it's a good thing I was proactive. You do remember how all of that turned out, don't you?"

She gave me another look.

"I mean, it wasn't my best moment," I continued. "If I had it to do over again, I would have handled it differently. I can see where it might seem weird."

"I just thought I'd put that warning out there."

Usually, I felt better after talking to Jamie. But, right now, I felt worse. Her warning was an ominous cloud hanging over my head, reminding me how things could go wrong.

Because I was the girl who always tried too hard to do everything right.

And sometimes that worked to my detriment.

I sat in the parking lot for a moment after meeting with Jamie and closed my eyes. I pictured Sarah leaving her last class. I imagined her heading toward the office, toward the doors she would exit from for parent pickup. But somewhere along the way, something had shifted.

She'd changed directions, gone to the student parking lot, and gotten into the car with someone else. Had she remembered something—a prior meeting, maybe? Had she gotten a phone call? Or had she passed someone who'd lured her away?

And the even more burning question was: Who could that person be she'd gotten in the car with?

Her friends didn't know anything—supposedly, at least.

She had a secret social media account set up. But I hadn't seen anything suspicious there other than Cameron.

What about her phone? How had Sarah gotten it? Who paid for it? The girl didn't have much money, and she would have to pay at least twenty a month for a burner phone . . . right? So where had she gotten that money?

I rubbed my temples. I had so many questions and so few answers. As I opened my eyes, the bright September sunlight hit them, causing me to squint.

Her frantic phone call to me began replaying in my head, and my heart ached when I thought about the fear in her voice. She'd asked me for help, and I intended on giving it to her.

If only I knew where to go next . . .

My phone rang, and my breath caught as I looked at the screen. Was it Sarah?

I released the air in my lungs when I realized it

wasn't. I didn't recognize the number, but I answered anyway.

"Ms. Holly?" a young-sounding female said on the other line.

I gripped the phone harder and sat up in my seat. "Yes? Who is this?"

"This is Allison. Sarah's friend."

"Yes, Allison. Hi. What's going on?"

"I . . . uh, I thought of something, and I thought I should tell you about it."

My pulse spiked. "Okay, go ahead, Allison. What's going on?"

"First, Sarah did have a phone," she started. "I'm sorry I didn't mention it sooner."

"I heard. Do you know where she got it or how she was paying for it?"

Allison remained quiet for a moment before clearing her throat. "Well, that's kind of what this is about. You see, there was this man who came to school. He was promoting this fundraiser thing so all the students could make money for extracurricular activities at the school. Sarah and I both thought it was stupid since neither of us participate in after-school activities."

"Go on." I could totally see the two of them having that conversation. I might even smile about it if the situation wasn't so grim right now.

"Anyway, Sarah ran into this guy who was in charge of the fundraisers in the hallway afterward, and they started talking. He was a real salesman. You know the type? He was a talker and could make anyone feel like a long-time friend."

Yes, I did know the type. "I do."

"Sarah jokingly mentioned something about fundraising for herself to pay her bills. She was trying to be funny. But this guy—the fundraiser man—mentioned that he knew a way she might be able to earn some money."

Suddenly, nothing else mattered but this conversation. "Allison, when did this happen?"

"It was only two weeks ago or so."

"Did she say anything else? Maybe about meeting him or something?" I held my breath as I waited for her response. Maybe this was the lead we'd been searching for.

"He got her phone number, and I think they were texting about the job. Sarah seemed excited. She wanted her own money, to feel like she could do something on her own."

My throat felt swollen as I prepared myself to ask my next question. "What kind of job, Allison?"

"I'm not sure. She didn't say. She only said it was easy money, and it was the answer to a lot of her prayers."

I closed my eyes, trying to drive out the worst-case scenarios that played in my mind. No, I had to stay positive. I couldn't let my thoughts go there. Not yet. "Why didn't you tell us this earlier, Allison?"

"Because Sarah made me promise not to." Allison's voice broke. "I'm sorry, Ms. Holly. But Sarah's been gone a whole day now, and I'm worried. I figured at first that she just took off to do the job, and she'd reappear. But now she's not at school today and . . .I don't know. I've been so worried that I just left class and went into the bathroom so I could call you."

"Have you seen this man since then?" I gripped my phone so hard that my knuckles ached. This was a lead, yes. But it wasn't exactly what I wanted to hear.

"No, I haven't. I'm . . . I'm sorry, Ms. Holly. Please help my friend."

"You've been a big help, Allison. Thank you for sharing this." I ended the call and dialed Chase's number. He had to know about this. Now.

CHAPTER 13

I ARRIVED at Hill Crest High at the same time Chase did. We met up from opposite sidewalks before walking side by side toward the front entry. I hastened my steps to match his.

"This could be our first lead, Chase."

"I hope it is."

My hastened steps turned into an all-out jog as I tried to keep up with Chase. He pushed his way inside the school and past the security checkpoint with just a flash of his badge. I had to stop and sign in. Of course.

By the time I got to the office, Chase was already talking to the principal. Who knew what I might have missed?

"Joe Richardson?" Principal Hamlin said. "You think Joe has something to do with this?"

Chase shifted on this side of the front counter. "I'm not sure, but I'd like to talk to him."

Hamlin shook her head. "But Joe is the nicest guy. I just can't see him having anything to do with Sarah's disappearance."

"Please, ma'am. His contact information." Chase's voice held a touch of irritation, but probably no one noticed it but me.

She finally nodded. "I'll get it for you."

Chase straightened, his hands still pressed against the counter and an annoyed expression on his face. I could read that he was getting impatient with all of this. Instead of talking or saying anything, I stayed quiet and gave him space.

Principal Hamlin returned a moment later with a paper in her hands. "Here you go."

Chase took the paper and glanced at the number. "Does this Joe guy hang around the school often?"

"Not often. He makes his rounds among all the area schools so he can promote his fundraising programs. They're some of the most productive we've had here at the school. We raised ten thousand dollars last year for the school's sports and arts programs."

"So he came two weeks ago to promote this?" Chase clarified.

"That's right. He did a school assembly, like he always does. Then he returned a week later to do a follow-up and check in. The forms for this program were due yesterday, so he returned."

"Wait . . ." I said. "He was here yesterday? The day Sarah disappeared?"

Principal Hamlin nodded. "Yes, I suppose he was. I didn't think anything about it. Why would I? Everyone who works in any capacity at this school goes through a background check, Joe included."

"I'm going to pay him a visit now." Chase started toward the door.

I followed closely on his heels. I wasn't missing this.

Chase didn't invite me to ride with him, but I'd climbed into the front passenger seat of his car anyway.

"I'll stay out of your way," I promised. I felt like a broken record every time I said that—as I should. I said it a lot.

"I know how well that's worked out in the past."

I would be offended, but his words were true. Again.

He typed a few things into the computer perched between the front seats and a moment later we took off toward Joe Richardson's place. Tension built inside me with every second that passed.

Was this it? Was there a predator working within the school system? I wasn't naïve enough to think it couldn't happen, but it still made me sick to my stomach to think about.

I pulled myself from my stupor and grabbed my phone. I searched for any information I could find on this Joe Richardson guy. Numerous social media sites popped up when I typed in his name, presenting me with a gold mine of information.

Joe Richardson was twenty-nine years old. He was from Brooklyn, New York. He had a full head of dark hair that was combed back away from his face and a million-dollar smile. In most of his online photos, he was pictured beside a different beautiful woman, with what mostly looked like clubs or bars in the background.

I looked through his messages and posts, but I didn't see anything that indicated he was trouble. A partier? Yes. Narcissist? Possibly. But what else lurked beneath his sparkling façade?

"What did you find?" Chase glanced over at me.

It was like he didn't even have to ask. He just knew that I'd been doing research on this guy.

I gave him the basic stats first before lowering my phone. "Joe looks like one of those charismatic types who could sell water to people in a flood. There wasn't anything to indicate he was up to no good. But I have my suspicions."

"Maybe this will be our first real lead. We desperately need something."

"Yes, we do. That's what I'm hoping."

We pulled to a stop in front of an apartment complex located near downtown. It was actually an old warehouse that had been cut up into industrial housing units. I was sure people paid top dollar to live here, probably in a studio that cost more than what I made in a month, all for a place barely big enough for a bed.

Chase parked on the street outside, and I followed him up three flights of stairs until he stopped at door 312. His fist knocked against the burgundy paint that covered the thick door.

I held my breath, hoping and praying we'd finally get some answers.

A moment later, Joe opened the door wearing nothing but a . . . bathrobe?

Chase flashed his badge. "Detective Chase Dexter, and this is . . . my colleague Holly. I have some questions for you."

Joe's face went pale—as did most people's when a detective confronted them at their front door. He reached for the doorframe and stared at Chase.

"What's this about?" he asked.

"Can we come in?" Chase nodded to the apartment beyond him.

Joe glanced over his shoulder and cringed. "It's better if you don't."

My heart spiked. Was that because he had Sarah inside? Because Joe had something to hide?

Chase seemed to follow my train of thought and peered beyond Joe. "Is there any reason we can't come in?"

Joe shook his head a little too fast. "Just because I just got out of the shower, and I'm feeling indecent. Plus, my place is messy."

Chase's jaw clenched. "This is important, Mr. Richardson."

"Fine." Joe pushed the door open with an annoyed puff of air shooting from his nose. "Come on. But I don't have much time."

We stepped inside, and I quickly glanced around. His apartment was just as small as I'd assumed and just as messy as he'd claimed. What might be a minimalistic paradise to some was overcome by clutter and poor housekeeping. Plus, it smelled like dirty socks.

"You have somewhere to go?" Chase's voice sounded rock hard and unbreakable.

"I have a date tonight, if you must know."

Chase leveled his gaze with him. "It's not with a four-teen-year-old girl, is it?"

Joe's eyes widened. "What? What are you talking about? Of course not. It's with Cassandra, a waitress at a bar two blocks from here. Now, would you care to explain to me what's going on?"

"A student from Hill Crest High has gone missing," Chase said. "We need to ask you a few questions."

"What would I have to do with that?" Joe sounded honestly appalled as he stared Chase down.

"We heard you were texting with this student."

Joe's bottom lip dropped open, and he finally shook his head—though barely. "Why would I text a student?"

"That's what we're hoping you'd tell us," Chase said.

I stepped forward, already not liking this guy. "Did you purposefully choose to work in the school system to live out some kind of sick fantasy?"

Joe turned to Chase, his gaze even more appalled now. "I'm not that kind of guy, and I resent the implication."

"That's what we're thinking right now," Chase said. "So you better start talking before I arrest you and your date is permanently canceled. Why were you texting Sarah Anderson?"

"Sarah? Sarah is missing?"

Chase narrowed his eyes. "That's correct. Why were you texting her? What was this easy way of making some extra money?"

"It's not what it sounds like." Joe's voice inched up, like he was getting more and more nervous by the minute.

"Then what is it?"

He threw his hands in the air, and I had to look away, fearful that bathrobe would come undone with his dramatics. "I did tell her about a job, but it's not what you're thinking. I have a friend with a company that pays people to do things on the internet."

"Do things on the internet?" I screeched, my mind going to terrible places.

"Not those kinds of things! All they have to do is click some things on different websites. It's like a product tester. It's easy, and they get ten dollars an hour."

Chase looked like he liked this guy less and less all the time. "Do you often recruit kids from the schools you frequent to do these jobs?"

"No, I don't. But Sarah was talking to me about needing some money, so it seemed like a natural thing to do."

A wave of disgust washed through me. "You had no qualms about getting a fourteen-year-old's phone number?"

"Only because it was for a job opportunity."

"That sounds like a great cover story," Chase said.

"It's not a cover story! I promise. I haven't seen Sarah since I got her phone number that day. I sent her the information, and she was in touch with my friend after that. I had no contact."

"What's this friend's name?"

"Earl Marks. Call him. He'll tell you."

"I'll definitely be calling him." Chase looked unconvinced that Joe was telling him the truth, though. "Where were you yesterday at 2:30 when school ended?"

"I was at the gym. People can verify I was there. I did not abduct a high school student."

"We'll need the name of the gym," Chase said.

"Of course. Anything to prove I'm innocent."

"You care if I look through your apartment then?" Chase asked.

Joe tensed. "I'd prefer you didn't."

"Is that because you're hiding someone here?" Chase started toward the door in the distance.

"Wait! No. It's not like you think."

Chase didn't stop. He jerked open the door.

And a woman was standing there, draped in a towel.

But she wasn't Sarah.

No, it was Sarah's teacher, Ms. Baldwin.

CHAPTER 14

"IT'S a business where you click things on the internet and get paid for it," Chase muttered to the two other detectives gathered around his desk.

I sat in the hallway outside his office, listening to the conversation between him and other people on his team.

I would have driven home or gone to do my own research, but I supposed this was the downside of riding along when I wasn't welcome. I hadn't been able to pick up my car, so now I was at the police station and at Chase's mercy.

I couldn't stop thinking about Joe Richardson, though.

Was he telling the truth?

That was what Chase and his colleagues were trying to figure out now.

We'd left Joe—and Ms. Baldwin—in the capable hands

of the crime-scene unit. Chase had searched the place for evidence but hadn't found anything. Joe Richardson had allowed the search with no reservations once he'd realized how guilty he looked.

As that had taken place, Ms. Baldwin had been a rambling mess. Apparently, she'd met Joe at school two weeks ago, and they'd gone out a couple times. She hadn't been at school today because of a dentist appointment, and she'd swung by Joe's on the way home.

Earl Marks sat in an interrogation room across the building. Another detective was taking a turn with him, but Chase apparently wasn't convinced he was involved in this.

"How do you even get money by clicking on links on these websites?" another detective asked. "Makes no sense to me."

I thought the detective's name was Hastings. I knew he'd worked with Chase on past cases.

"It's one of these sites where people get paid per times people click on various links," Chase said. "Scammers hire people to click different online ads, even though they're not really interested in the product. The advertiser pays out money per click, so some people have found ways to work the system."

"Is it illegal?" Detective Hastings asked.

I was just going to assume that was his name.

"It's in litigation," Chase said.

Another officer walked into the office—the office and discussion I'd been turned away from. I was certain Chase was trying to teach me a lesson right now.

"Earl Marks said he did hire Sarah Anderson, but she hadn't started work yet," the officer said. "He found a copy of all of their text conversations, and we were able to print them out for review."

I straightened, leaning closer to hear better.

"Anything?" Chase asked.

"No, everything lines up, and I didn't see anything inappropriate."

"Good to know."

"I also checked Joe's phone records and his computer messages," the officer continued. "It appears that his story checks out. The only contact he had with our missing girl was passing along his friend's information."

My heart sank. I'd been so hopeful that maybe we had finally gotten our first lead.

But now we were back to zero.

I leaned my head against the cement wall behind me. *Sarah, where are you?*

With every minute that passed, she seemed to slip further away.

And the feeling in my gut only became tighter and emptier.

After an hour of eavesdropping, I stood. I couldn't do this anymore. This little time out had come to an end.

The crew in the office had only been talking about verifying everything they'd learned, to make it official. I appreciated that they were thorough, but I could clearly see this was leading nowhere except paperwork.

I stuck my head into the office and got Chase's attention. "I'm going to call Uber."

"If you can wait a few minutes, I'll take you back to your car," Chase said. "Or I can have a patrol officer do it."

"That's okay. I'll figure out something myself." I didn't want to wait a moment longer than necessary. Nope, I was done.

I took a step toward the door, but Chase appeared from his office and met me in the hallway. His towering frame and close positioning made me crane my neck upward in order to see his eyes and find out what he wanted.

"We're going to find her." His voice sounded low and soothing.

He was trying to cheer me up, but my heart was too heavy right now to feel lifted. In fact, I was downright fatigued. "Thanks for everything you're doing, Chase."

His eyes showed worry and concern as they crinkled at the edges. "Holly . . ."

"Really, I'll be okay. Some time alone will be good for me. Besides, being up all night is starting to take its toll.

Maybe I'll take a nap. Or maybe I'll just grab some coffee —except not from here."

That got a smile out of him. "If I hear anything, I'll let you know."

"Same here."

Uber took me back to my car at Hill Crest High. But instead of going home, I headed down to the Family Services office. I wanted to talk to Sarah's social worker. I didn't even know why. I didn't think Kathy would have any more information to give me. But I still wanted to speak with someone who might understand what was going on.

Since I used to work there, I skipped the red tape and went straight to her office, stopping to talk to a few old friends on my way. Seeing them perked me up ever so slightly.

Kathy stood when she saw me. Instead of saying anything for a greeting, she skirted around the desk and pulled me into a hug. Kathy had been here three years when I started, and she'd taken me under her wing and helped show me the ropes.

Since then, she'd gotten married and she had two little kids of her own at home. She didn't look as young as she once had—then again, who did? Her hair was bobbed to her chin, she had bags under her eyes, and her clothing was often stained.

"How are you doing?" She pulled away and took a seat in front of her desk. She nudged out the second blue pleather seat beside her, indicating I should sit. "You don't look good."

I really should have gotten that coffee, apparently.

"I've been better," I told her, taking a seat.

"Any updates?"

I shook my head. "Every time we think we have a lead, it turns out to be nothing."

"I'm so sorry to hear that, Holly. I can imagine this is hard for you. It's been hard on all of us here, as well." Though Kathy said the words, something about them didn't exactly ring true. I couldn't put my finger on what, however.

Kathy was Sarah's social worker. She should be just as concerned as I was. I mean, I realized she was over-worked with more children than she could adequately oversee. I'd been in her shoes, and I knew the daily struggles she faced.

But where was the sincere concern? The concern that kept her up at night. That caused her to put in late hours. That made her determination kick in.

"Why aren't you more worried?" I finally asked.

Kathy drew her head back, looking offended by my words. "Well, of course, I'm worried."

"Finding Sarah doesn't appear to be urgent for anyone here. Have things changed that much since I left this office? Aren't the children your first concern?"

"Holly, you know we care about these kids." She sounded insulted—as she should be.

But I wasn't ready to let this drop. "Then what is it?"

She let out a sigh and grabbed a folder from the desk beside her. "The truth is—and I think you know this—foster kids are prone to running away."

I blinked. "You think Sarah ran away?"

"I think there's a good chance of it."

"Why would she run away?" She didn't know Sarah like I did. She had no right to draw those conclusions.

"Why does any foster kid run away? It's what they've done their entire lives. They've been shuffled about with no real place to call home—especially once they reach their teens and if they've been in the system for any extended amount of time, nowhere feels like home, and there's nothing to keep them tied down."

"Sarah wasn't like that." I heard Kathy's words, but I couldn't believe them.

"Holly, if you were able to step back from this, you'd know my words are true." She opened the folder. "Just this year alone, we've had five kids in the system run away."

"Five?" Why didn't I remember this from my time as a social worker? Had I been naïve? I didn't know.

I glanced over at the open folder and quickly scanned the names there before Kathy shut it again, as if she hadn't intended on sharing so much.

"That's right. Five. Mostly teenagers. One ran away from her foster home. Another left school early and never came back. One openly fought with her foster parents and walked out. It's the same old story time and time again."

"I don't want to believe that. Who's fighting for those kids?"

"We do what we can, Holly. You know what our case-load is."

It sounded like an excuse to me. "But those kids deserve a voice."

"They're walking away from the support we give them. It's an uphill battle. They're tired of being under our jurisdiction and want freedom. They think they can do better on their own."

"Not Sarah."

Kathy let out a sigh, obviously frustrated that I didn't see things her way. "We're cooperating with the police all we can. There's not much else more we can do."

I stood and nodded. "Thanks for meeting with me."

But I left feeling worse than when I'd come.

CHAPTER 15

AS SOON AS I got back into my car, my phone rang.

It was Drew.

Instead of feeling my spirits lift, they sagged at the thought of talking to him. Why was that?

Probably because I didn't want to deal with any relationship drama. Which was weird, because Drew and I hadn't had any relationship drama until yesterday. And now I felt bogged down by it. Then again, everything was making me feel bogged down lately.

I plastered on my most friendly voice as I answered. "Hey, you."

"Hey, sweetie. Look, I know you have a lot going on, so you can say no. But you'd originally promised to help me out here at the funeral home this evening since my mom has that retirement party to go to."

I rested my forehead against my steering wheel. That's right. How had I forgotten?

It had even been on my to-do list . . . the one I hadn't even thought about since I found out Sarah was gone.

"I'll understand if you can't make it," Drew said.

Could I make it? I didn't *want* to make it. But I didn't actually have anything else scheduled—except trying to find Sarah. But I didn't know yet what my next step was, which most likely meant I'd only be sitting around my house worrying.

"I'll be there," I said, pulling myself together. "What time again?"

"6:30."

That gave me just enough time to run home and get cleaned up. To maybe not look like such a corpse myself. Two people had already mentioned how tired I looked.

I changed into a dark blue A-line dress, grabbed an apple with some almond butter for a quick dinner, and I was out the door faster than the boogeyman could say boo.

But as I pulled up to the funeral home, the sense of dread that swelled in my gut was enough to make me want to throw up. I hated this place.

I never admitted that out loud to Drew. This was his livelihood. His family business. Likely, it would be his legacy.

But every time I stepped inside, so many bad memories hit me. Memories of doing this for my dad. Of looking at him in a casket at the end of a center aisle, his body lifeless and waxy—nothing at all like the vibrant man I remembered.

I recalled the platitudes by well-wishers who intended their best. I remembered trying to hold back my own tears and be strong throughout the ceremony, only so I could let everything out when I was alone later within the privacy of my bedroom.

Bad memories. Some of the worst ones of my life, for that matter.

And the people coming here this evening would be making their own horrible memories as they laid their loved one to rest.

It was my job to greet them. To help them. To be a shadow in the background who only emerged when I could offer some kind of comfort or practical service.

If I married Drew, was this what the rest of my life would look like? Helping him here? Learning to live with this misery?

I swallowed hard and stepped inside, ready to do my job. A job everyone thought I would be perfect for. One that required me to be polite and compassionate and well-mannered.

So why did I feel so ill-equipped?

I nearly fell into my couch when I got home at nine that evening.

Working at the funeral home had been just as bad as I'd thought it would be.

I'd left Drew there finishing up his responsibilities. He'd offered to take me out to a late dinner if I waited for him, but I was too exhausted, and he seemed to understand that.

Just as I closed my eyes with a cup of chamomile tea cooling on my end table, someone knocked at the door. My back muscles tightened. Who would possibly be stopping by at this time of the evening?

"Holly, it's me. Chase. Can I come in?"

I drew in a sharp breath when I opened the door and saw Chase there. I'd known it was him, of course. But just seeing him there . . . soaking in his broad physique. His warm blue eyes. His familiar face.

He'd obviously gone home because he was now wearing jeans and a nice blue henley. Based on the slight dampness in his hair, he may have even showered.

I was tempted to lean closer to confirm if I was right, to smell his fresh aftershave or the minty shampoo he always used.

But that wasn't happening.

I cleared my throat instead. "I didn't expect to see you here. Not at this hour."

He frowned. "You looked discouraged earlier. I wanted to check on you."

I let him close the door himself, and I went back to the couch and nearly collapsed on it again. He sat in the chair beside me, keeping his distance. Physically, at least. His gaze made me feel like I was wrapped in his embrace.

But I wasn't. Nor did I want to be, I reminded myself. We were friends, and I could handle this. It wasn't either/or. We didn't have to date or be strangers—there was middle ground. It was just going to take some adjustment.

"I'm okay," I finally said.

"Are you sure?"

I sat up and let out a long breath. "I just got home from helping out at the funeral home. It's emotionally exhausting for me to do that. It's so much grief to be around. But I know what grief is like, so I should be the perfect one for that part-time job."

Chase studied me long enough that I shifted uncomfortably. "You know, just because you can do something doesn't mean you're supposed to do it."

My spine stiffened. "What's that mean?"

"I'm just saying that I know you hate to fail at anything, but it's okay sometimes to not do something just because you don't want to."

"What are you talking about? There are plenty of things I'm not good at. Like sports."

"Yeah, but I'm talking about these etiquette-y, polite type of things that you usually excel at." He waved his hand in the air like he couldn't think of all the proper terms.

"What are you talking about?" I repeated myself, but only because I totally wasn't following what he was saying. At all.

Chase's voice sounded low as he spoke again. "Holly, you hate working at the funeral home. Yes, you *can* do it. And yes, you *could* do it exceedingly well if you set your mind to it. But it's okay to not do it. To not enjoy it. To acknowledge that it sucks the life out of you."

Chase was the last person I should be getting advice from—for so many reasons. But I wanted to hear what he had to say, regardless. "I never said I hated it."

"You don't have to. You look lifeless after you do it." His gaze seemed to sear into my soul.

"Chase—"

He raised a hand in surrender and leaned back. "Look, I know it's none of my business. I know I should stay out of it. I just hate to see you like this."

"Well, I appreciate your concern, but I'm handling things fine." I shifted, suddenly feeling way more exposed than I wanted to feel. "Now, why did you stop by again? Are there any updates?"

"No updates. I really did come by just to check on you."

That was awfully nice of him. "I feel like we're never going to find answers."

"I know. Be patient."

"I can't be patient. Do you know why?" Before Chase could answer, I stood and walked into the kitchen. I opened the fridge and reached in to grab a handful of insulin and proclaim Sarah's health was in danger.

But I couldn't because . . . the fridge was empty.

CHAPTER 16

"YOU'RE SAYING all her diabetes medications were in that refrigerator earlier today?" Chase clarified, staring at the empty shelf in front of him.

I shook my head, fighting my rising panic. "No, I didn't check today. I checked the supplies yesterday."

Chase shifted. "So, at some point between then and now, someone came in and took Sarah's diabetes supplies."

"That's how it appears." As the words left my mouth, I shook my head. Conclusions fought to surface in my mind, but I didn't want them to. I couldn't handle them right now. "Let me check her bedroom also, just to make sure nothing is missing there."

I rushed to her room and opened her drawers, her

closet. Nothing was missing. I paused and pinched the skin between my eyes. What was going on here?

"Holly, there's only one person I can think of who would do this. Sarah did have a key to the house, right?"

I looked up and saw that he'd followed me. He lingered in the doorway, watching me. "She did. But—"

"Holly, Sarah is the only one who makes sense."

"But that would mean . . ." I couldn't even finish my statement, couldn't bring life to my thoughts.

But Chase had no qualms about it. "Maybe she did run away."

I shook my head, the words feeling like an assault on my ears. "I don't believe that."

"I just don't want you to be disappointed if the conclusion of all this isn't what you want."

I leaned against the counter, feeling another wave of exhaustion wash over me. "Chase, everyone needs someone in their life who'll go that extra mile. Who believes in them. I can't give up on her."

"Like you gave up on me."

His words spread across the room like radiation spread after a bomb drop. Had he just said that? Was that really what he thought? The first flicker of anger lit inside me.

"That's not fair, Chase. You were the one who wouldn't commit. I gave you plenty of chances."

"I loved you, Holly." He stepped closer, his voice low, intimate, and pleading.

"But not enough to commit," I repeated, needing to drive home that point. Had he forgotten his role in all of this?

"I just needed time."

"If we were still dating, you still wouldn't be ready, Chase. It's like the Israelites wandering in the desert. That's what I felt like—like I was walking in circles. If you didn't know what you wanted after we dated for almost a year, then I'm not your girl." My words had punch— punch I hadn't counted on. But I'd been wrestling with my choices, and this conversation probably should have taken place much earlier.

He stepped back and ran a hand through his hair, an obvious struggle going on inside him. "I just didn't want to start our marriage with so much baggage, Holly. It didn't seem fair to you."

He had been married before, and it had ended badly. I could see where that would make him think twice. But . . .

"The truth is, we're always going to have baggage, Chase. You and me both. That's what life experiences will do to you, and it doesn't get any better as we get older. Nope, we have more experiences and more baggage every time we get hurt or someone lets us down or a plan doesn't go the way we anticipated."

He dipped his head and released a long, low breath. "I'm sorry. I shouldn't have brought it up."

I wanted to reach for him, but I remembered my boundaries. Instead, I raised my chin, keeping my voice compassionate yet firm. "I am dating Drew now."

"And he seems like he's really good for you." His voice cracked.

"He is."

Chase nodded toward the door, resignation showing in the slope of his shoulders. "I should go."

I nodded, wanting to stop him. To tell him everything would be okay. To . . . I really didn't know what. Just *something*. Instead, I said, "Goodnight, Chase."

He stepped away, and I felt like the door to our past was slamming closed. A wave of grief washed over me.

"Chase?" I called.

He turned, a flicker of hope in his eyes.

"We're always friends, right?"

"Of course, Holly."

"It's not going to be weird if I talk to you about this investigation?" Of all the things I could say, that's what I had chosen? I mentally kicked myself.

"It will be, but we should push through it."

I smiled at his honesty. "Okay, then. We'll talk later."

After Chase left and after I'd finished my lukewarm tea, I lay in bed. I was unable to sleep, even though my body was worn down and ready to break.

There was too much on my mind, and it cycled like a twenty-four-hour news station on a five-minute talking rotation.

Had Sarah really come back while I'd been gone and retrieved her medication? Had she watched the house, waiting for me to leave, so she could get inside without being caught?

I had been convinced that she'd been abducted. But she was the only person I could think of who would steal her prescriptions. She made the most sense. So maybe all of this was for nothing, and Sarah really had run away.

If she did, would that change my stance on this investigation? I still thought Sarah needed to be found. But maybe she wasn't in quite so much danger.

I didn't know.

Next, my mind bounced to my conversation with Chase. How dare he say I'd given up on him? I'd stood by patiently for longer than I should have. If Chase had given me any indication that he would one day be ready to settle down, I would have probably stayed and waited. But he hadn't.

So I'd broken up with him. It had been the right thing.

But if it was the right thing, why did I feel so bad right now?

And what about his proclamation concerning me working at the funeral home? Was I really sacrificing my own happiness to try and support Drew? If so, could I see myself doing that for the rest of my life? I didn't know if I could do that for the rest of my life.

Finally, I threw the covers off and went to my laptop, which I'd left on my dresser. I grabbed it, pulled it into my lap, and stared at the screen for a minute. I wasn't even sure what I wanted to search for, I just knew I wanted to do *something* to distract myself from the tortured thoughts repeating themselves over and over.

I pulled up a list of saved tabs I had on my internet browser. Whenever I had the time—or got the obsession in my head—I liked to research a few loose threads in my life.

The first tab was dedicated to the death of Chase's brother, Hayden. I knew I should stay out of the investigation. But ever since I'd heard Chase tell his story, I'd looked for information on Hayden's death, trying to find some clue the police had missed. I'd come up with nothing.

The next tab was information on my dad. My mom had discovered that he'd actually been adopted. The adoption was closed, so we didn't know much about his biological family. However, my mom had posted on a message board and a mysterious stranger had shown up in our lives, only to equally as mysteriously disappear.

On occasion, I still felt like someone was watching me, and I wondered if it involved my dad's bio family. I searched for information on them on nights when I couldn't sleep, but I hadn't found anything significant yet. I hoped something might pop up one day and give me the answers I sought.

I turned back to the computer and started to type something but stopped. I didn't even know where to start looking for Sarah or what to search for or what to do. I drew a blank, and my fingers, unfortunately, hadn't taken on a mind of their own and led me to where my conscious mind hadn't.

Instead, I clicked on Chatbook. I hardly ever checked in there. I hadn't even wanted to create a page, but I set one up at the urging of Jamie. *Everyone should have a page,* she'd told me. However, I never posted. I did, on occasion, enjoy keeping up with people from my past and hearing about their accomplishments and children and weddings, etc.

I saw I had ten new messages. Out of curiosity, I clicked on them. Most were nothing important. Spam or chain mail. One was from an old college friend. However, she included a link for some health aid she'd just started selling, which seemed to dilute her sincerity about wanting to catch up.

The last message I read—which just happened to be the newest one—was from . . . Rae Harding? Hadn't

Sarah's made-up name been Sarah Rae? Was this somehow connected?

I swallowed hard before clicking on it.

My eyes widened when I read the message.

Don't look for me. I've decided to do things my way. You were good to me, Ms. Holly, but I'm ready to get out of the system. Please, let me go. It's time.

CHAPTER 17

I SAT STRAIGHT up in bed the next morning with sweat covering my forehead. I glanced around, feeling as if I'd missed *something*. Some catastrophic event. I waited to remember it, for the episode to hit me like a runaway Mack truck on an icy day.

Instead, all I saw was daylight streaming through my curtains. Peace. Serenity. The familiar comforts of home.

What in the world . . . ?

I ran a hand over my face.

I'd been dreaming, I realized. And something in my dream had made sense in real life, connecting my unconsciousness to reality and bridging the two in a way only dreams and sleep could do. But what had that bridging been?

I closed my eyes and desperately tried to remember.

Images of bumblebees hit me. Then to-do lists that were so long they wrapped around me until I couldn't breathe. Then running into a haunted house and being unable to get out.

No, none of those dreams were the ones I searched for.

Wait . . . I remembered!

I'd been seeing yard signs around town from people wanting to buy diabetic test strips for cash. Some were staked into the ground at corners. Others had been pinned on telephone poles or taped to streetlights.

The memory might be nothing.

But what if those thoughts were somehow tied in with Sarah? Was I reaching too far? I didn't know, but it was an idea worth exploring.

I scrambled from bed, grabbed my laptop again, and hopped online. I typed in "diabetic test strips for sale" and a slew of results came up. I clicked on the first one I found from a respectable news site and began reading.

Apparently, these test strips were expensive in the stores—sometimes up to eighty dollars for a five-day supply. Sometimes insurance carriers covered it, but sometimes they didn't. Because of this, some people purchased second-rate or black-market test strips instead. These could be found on sites like Amazon or eBay. Instead of costing nearly two dollars per strip, they were being sold for about twenty cents per strip—a significant savings.

Who sold these strips, though? I wondered. I kept reading.

From what I understood, sometimes people on Medicaid or Medicare received either too many strips or they undertested themselves, leading to an overage. Sometimes these same people needed money themselves and saw selling the strips as a way of earning some quick cash. Other times, the strips being sold were from unreliable suppliers in other countries or were damaged and unable to be sold in stores, though they worked.

Dealers posted signs around town or ads on the internet, advertising their desire to buy people's extra test strips. These dealers then resold the diabetic supplies to those who needed them, at a cheaper price—but high enough that they could make a profit.

I leaned back and tried to let that new information sink in.

Had Sarah figured out a way to earn extra money by selling those strips? She wouldn't have come up with that idea on her own. I didn't think so, at least. She wasn't the entrepreneurial type. No, she liked to fly under the radar, to act more as a follower than a leader.

I rubbed my temples, trying to think this through. I could be way off base, but what if I wasn't? What if she was trying to spread her wings, just as that message last night had indicated? She couldn't do that on her own. No, she'd need money.

Sarah and Cameron Penki had apparently met because they were both diabetics. Even though the police had cleared him, what if he'd talked her into earning some extra cash this way?

Or how about Joe? Though there was no evidence he was guilty, he could have seen an opportunity to exploit a young girl with health concerns.

The police may have cleared those two, but that didn't mean they weren't hiding something and that they weren't in some way involved.

The diabetic test strip theory could be worth exploring.

Now the question was: Did I call Chase and tell him about this? Or did I try to find answers on my own?

I also remembered the message I'd received from Sarah. Should I tell him about that, as well?

I hadn't called him last night to share the information. No, I'd feared Chase would call off the investigation. I couldn't let that happen . . . mostly because something in the wording of that message didn't ring true to Sarah and how she said things. I couldn't identify exactly what it was.

I only knew this was far from being over.

～

After chewing on the idea for a while, I called Chase. He told me the diabetic test strips were a good lead and that he would look into it. Of course I wanted to be there when he did, but Chase didn't offer this time, and I didn't press my luck—especially after our conversation last night.

I also decided to tell him about the message I'd received. He told me he'd have his team look into that social media profile and see if they could glean anything from it.

I got dressed and went out to my car, figuring I might be able to do a little investigating on my own. I wanted to track down some of the phone numbers from those signs around town. I was also considering doing a search for Sarah's mom. If the police couldn't find her, I knew there was little chance I could. But it would at least be worth a try.

Instead, I froze on my driveway.

My tires had been slashed.

What?

I squatted beside my car and examined the gashes. All four of them. One in each tire.

I sighed.

Had someone been trying to send a message?

Whose toes had I stepped on?

Cameron?

Joe?

Was there someone else I was missing?

A headache started to form at my temples. Nothing was ever simple. Now I had to figure out how to get anywhere today, how to get this fixed, and where to get the money.

I started to call Chase again but stopped myself.

Why in the world had I thought of Chase right now?

I shook the thought off and dialed Drew's number instead.

"Hey, beautiful. To what honor do I owe this early morning call?" His voice sounded cheerful and welcoming, and I was grateful to hear it.

I glanced at my watch and realized it was only 7:30. Thankfully, he was an early riser.

"I . . . uh, well, actually . . . my tires were slashed last night," I said.

"What?" The playfulness left his voice.

"It's true. I just discovered it."

"Did you call the police?"

The police? Yes, that would make sense. That was why Chase's image had come to my mind. I suppressed a nervous giggle, feeling a little better about my first instinct now that it made more sense.

"Not yet. I'm going to do that, though I doubt they'll be able to figure out who did this. It's pretty cut and dry, no pun intended."

"It's still a good idea to report it."

"I agree." Sometimes, those were the hardest words ever to say. They shouldn't be, however.

"Listen, let me change and I'll be right there," Drew said.

I sat on my front steps and let the sunlight bathe me in its glow for a moment. "You don't have work to do?"

"As a matter of fact, I don't. I was going to call you at eight to see if you wanted to do breakfast."

"Breakfast would be fantastic." Maybe it would help my life feel a little more normal.

"Great. You call the police. I'll come over. As soon as it's cleared, we can go buy some new tires and I'll change them for you."

"You're a real lifesaver." The fact that he'd drop everything for me meant a lot.

I ended the call, grateful that I had Drew in my life. I hoped I never forgot all the reasons why.

CHAPTER 18

THE POLICE ARRIVED BEFORE DREW. I recognized the officer they'd sent out as Ned Bishop. I'd worked with him before as a social worker, and I'd always thought the fifty-something officer was friendly and competent.

He took photos of my tires, asked questions like if I'd heard anything outside last night, and then he paused as we stood there on the cracked sidewalk leading to my porch. I could tell there was something on Officer Bishop's mind.

"Sorry to hear about you and Chase," he said.

"Thank you," I said.

"He always said you saw things from a different perspective, and that's what made you an asset to him when trying to solve various cases."

"He said that?" I questioned, unsure if I should believe him. Chase had never said that to me.

"He did. He said you were unique and that people related to you because they could see how much you cared. You should take that as a high compliment."

I swallowed hard, still trying to process. "I do. Believe me, I do."

Maybe Chase didn't think I was a hindrance to solving his cases after all. I'd like to think that I'd helped some—when I wasn't getting in his way. But I did love people, and I knew people tended to open up to me. I'd been an unofficial counselor to people throughout my life.

"He hasn't been himself the past few months, you know," Bishop said.

I swallowed hard, knowing I shouldn't ask any more questions, but more than a little curious about what he'd said. I finally settled on, "Is that right?"

"I think you were good for him. You brought out something in him, the way only the love of a good woman can do."

My curiosity turned to guilt. "Well, I'm sure he'll find someone else."

The officer let out a sigh, and his hands went to his waist, as if he'd said his piece and knew he needed to move on. "Okay, then. I've taken my report on your car—she's a beauty, by the way. I'll see what I can do. But I don't have high expectations that we're going to find anything here. Stuff like this happens all too often in this area, and the culprits are never found. They really leave no evidence behind."

"That's what I expected."

Drew arrived and joined us, putting his arm around my waist. He extended his hand toward Officer Bishop. "I'm Drew. Thanks for coming."

Officer Bishop looked at me, a slightly confused look on his face. He almost looked accusatory, like I was cheating on Chase by dating Drew.

"Right, right," he finally said. "No problem. I'll be on my way. Have a good day, you two."

As soon as he left, I turned to Drew, feeling shakier than I would like. I wasn't sure if it was because of the car, the conversation, or the fatigue that was plaguing me lately. "How about that breakfast? I could use some food right about now."

"Of course. I heard about this great little bistro not far from here. It just opened a few weeks ago. I thought we could try it out."

"Let's go." Anywhere away from here sounded good right now.

He led me to his cherry red '66 Mustang, opened the door for me, and waited until I was inside before getting inside himself. Yes, we'd bonded over our love for the classic car.

"You look beautiful." He glanced over at me and grinned.

"Thank you."

"You always look beautiful." Drew put the car into reverse and backed out of my driveway.

"And you're always so sweet." I couldn't ask for a more complimentary boyfriend.

We took off down the road. "Thanks again for filling in last night at the funeral home. It was such a huge help."

I remembered my conversation with Chase about it, and my stomach twisted. I hesitated, unsure how to respond. Did I tell him how much I hated it? Or should I just suck it up? I had bigger problems at the moment, I decided.

"Is everything okay?" Drew asked, glancing over at me.

I nodded, my default. "Yes, of course."

"You look tired."

Why did people keep saying that? I *was* tired. I hadn't slept well since Sarah disappeared.

We pulled up a few minutes later to a cute little bistro located in a revitalized part of town. It had an old brick storefront with flowerboxes filled with colorful pansies. Inside, it was small and cozy, with small wooden tables painted in various shades of green and blue. The scent of bacon and cinnamon filled the air, and soothing acoustic music played overhead.

I saved any deep questions until we were seated and I had my coffee. I ordered an egg-and-bacon sandwich on a croissant, and Drew got yogurt with granola and a fruit salad.

One of us chose wisely, and the other didn't. I'd never thought of myself as a stress eater, but apparently I was.

After the waitress left, I glanced through my eyelashes at Drew. He really was so handsome. And such a gentleman. The perfect material for a boyfriend and, one day, a husband.

If I gave him the right signals, he'd probably propose, and I could begin my happy ever after.

So why did I hold back? The question felt like it echoed inside my soul until an ache formed.

"What's the update on Sarah?" Drew spread his fabric napkin out over his lap with manners that would make Martha Stewart proud.

"Nothing yet," I told him, taking a sip of my coffee. "But we might have a lead."

I told him about my theory about the diabetic test strips.

When I finished, he made a face.

"What?" I asked, curious as to what he was thinking. "Do you think I'm reaching?"

"That seems drastic for some medical supplies."

"I didn't say it wasn't drastic. I'm just looking for answers, and all the other leads have run dry."

"I get that. But why not just break in and steal the supplies? Why would Sarah run away only to come back and get the strips and the insulin? Unless running away wasn't her original plan but more of an impulse?"

That was a good question. A great question, for that matter. Why go to such extreme measures? Had running been spontaneous, as Drew suggested? Under duress? I had so many questions still.

When I said nothing for a moment, Drew leaned closer. "Listen, I just don't think that following false leads should give you any more comfort than having no leads at all. I don't want to see you disappointed."

"I appreciate that. Maybe it was just a crazy theory."

He reached across the table and squeezed my hand. "Maybe the lead will go somewhere—somewhere you don't think, though. That's how these things always seem to work with you."

"It is, isn't it? I do hope it leads us somewhere. And I do think you may be right that Sarah might have left on her own accord. I hate to admit it." I told him about the message I'd received from Sarah last night.

"I know that's hard for you to swallow."

That was an understatement. "I thought I'd given her a better life."

"Some people walk away from the good life they had because they don't know any better."

"Why do people do that? Why leave a good thing for the unknown? I just don't get it."

Drew squeezed my hand again. "So many reasons, Holly. Sometimes it's fear. Sometimes it's a craving for the familiar. Sometimes they don't think they deserve the good."

I had to chew on that theory, but it seemed to make a lot of sense.

"Enough about me. How about you, Drew? Anything new?"

He shrugged. "No, I can't say there's anything new. I miss you."

I smiled. "I miss you too. Hopefully things will return to normal soon."

Our food came. Drew prayed, and we began eating.

But my heart still felt unsettled.

I didn't know if that would change until Sarah was found.

Back at my place after breakfast, Drew changed my tires —after we went to the store to purchase them. I'd pulled some money from a savings account to pay for it, but I hoped my insurance company would reimburse me.

I sat on my front porch and watched as Drew worked. I'd made lemonade, and I brought out some lemon-drizzled sugar cookies. I'd made them last week and had frozen them.

My mind wandered to Sarah and to the case.

Had Chase discovered anything yet? Had my theory held any merit? If not, what next? How would I find my foster daughter?

Until my car was fixed, I wouldn't be able to take off on my own and investigate.

Maybe it was better that way.

Drew came back over, wearing a white T-shirt with his khaki shorts. He had dirt smeared across his shirt and a sheen of sweat across his skin. The man always thought ahead, though, and he'd brought some old clothes to change into.

It was a different look for prim and proper Drew, but I liked it.

"All fixed," he said, wiping his hands.

"You're amazing."

He leaned toward me and pressed his lips into the side of my face.

"What was that for?" I sensed there was more to it than a sweet gesture.

"I realize I've been acting a little jealous lately, and I'm sorry. I know it's not cool."

"It's . . . it's okay."

He sat down beside me. "No, you're perfectly trust-worthy. I know you are. I shouldn't have reacted like that. It's just that with your and Chase's past . . ."

I swallowed even harder. "I know it's a bit much. But thank you for trusting me."

"You're about as trustworthy as they come."

I reached up and ran my fingers across Drew's smooth jaw. I soaked in his polished features. His perfect hair. His magazine-worthy smile and flawless olive skin. "You're a good man, Drew Williams."

"I try. You make me better."

He took a long drink of his lemonade. The moment ordinarily would feel perfect. A sunny day. Sitting on the porch. Drinking lemonade.

But this felt less than ideal. As hard as I tried to just be in the moment, my soul was unsettled. Sarah was missing, and the thought wouldn't leave my mind.

"I could see us doing this, Holly."

I glanced at him. "What do you mean? We are doing it. Right now."

He grinned and rested his hand on my knee. "No, I mean, I could see us doing this forever."

I felt my cheeks heat at the thought. Wasn't that what I wanted? "That would be nice, wouldn't it?"

"I think it would be more than nice."

He leaned in for another kiss, but his phone rang. He sighed, glanced at it, and frowned.

"I've got to go in. The life of a funeral director."

"Of course," I said. "One never knows when death will call."

My words echoed in my mind, a stoic reminder of just how uncertain life could be.

CHAPTER 19

AS SOON AS Drew left for work, I drove around and gathered the numbers from some of those diabetic test strip signs. Actually, they all ended up being the same number. I called it, but it went to voice mail, so I left a message.

After that, I did a picture search using the photo of Sarah's mom. I also got nowhere with that, which meant I was batting zero so far.

I leaned back into my couch and reflected on my conversation with Kathy yesterday. She said it wasn't that unusual for foster kids to disappear. I supposed, when I set my emotions aside, I did remember that happening on occasion. Back then, their disappearances just hadn't felt personal.

Kathy had held up that folder with a list of other

missing foster kids. I'd seen the names. I may have even committed those names to memory.

I turned back to my computer and typed in one of the names. Most foster kids didn't have much of an online presence, for privacy reasons. But the rules were changing. The world was changing. Quickly.

I found a couple of online mentions, but nothing significant.

I moved on to the second name. The girl, Avril White, had numerous social media pages. I clicked on her picture and squinted.

Why did she look so familiar?

The girl had dark hair that had been bleached blonde, and a gleam of defiance shone in her eyes. Her last post had been five months ago. That must be when she disappeared.

I clicked through several pictures, but I couldn't pinpoint why she seemed familiar to me.

Maybe this was all for nothing.

But that wasn't good enough for me.

Thankfully, my phone rang just then and pulled me from my misery. It was Chase.

"A couple of updates," he started.

"I'm all ears."

"We examined that other Chatbook page where the message was sent from. It was only created two days ago."

"That's strange."

"I know."

"Secondly, Cameron does have diabetes," Chase said. "We could find no evidence to indicate he might be stealing medical supplies to earn money. We're looking into him, though, just to verify his story. Another officer is tracking the GPS on his phone. That should tell us a lot about where he's been over the past few days."

"Oh." I couldn't hide the disappointment in my voice. We just needed one decent break in this case.

"It was a good theory, Holly."

I wasn't sure about that. Maybe I was reaching here, getting a little too desperate for answers.

"Are you guys still trying to find Sarah?" I asked.

That was my fear. That they'd think she ran, and that they'd give up on finding her. Could I live the rest of my life without answers? Was this what Chase felt like with his brother? The burden was greater than I'd imagined.

"Of course we're still looking for her. We're not giving up."

Relief whooshed through me, and I sagged into the couch cushions. "That's good."

"If you have any more ideas or leads, let me know. And what's this I hear about your tires being slashed?"

"The officer apprised you of the situation?" I remembered Officer Bishop's unusual interest in our love life—or lack thereof.

"He did. Bishop sometimes feels like a father to me. We talk quite a bit."

So the man had known what he was talking about when it came to Chase. Good to know.

"I don't suppose you have any idea who's responsible for your car?"

"I have no clue. I didn't hear a thing last night."

"Okay, well, stay safe. And if you need anything, let me know. Promise?"

"Promise."

Just as I ended the call, my doorbell rang.

Who now? I stood to find out.

"Ms. Baldwin?" I blinked, uncertain who I was seeing.

But, yes, it was Sarah's teacher. Her eyes were red-rimmed now, her hair pulled into a sloppy ponytail, and her hands wrung together in front of her. "Hi, Holly. I'm sorry to stop by unannounced and uninvited."

"It's . . . it's okay. But how did you know where I lived?"

"I just put your name in Google. Isn't that how everyone finds people?"

I shook my head, realizing I may have made that a little too easy for people. "Of course. What's going on?"

"Can I talk to you for a moment?"

"Come on in."

Ms. Baldwin stepped inside and her eyes went to the couch. I extended my hand back. "Have a seat. Can I get you some coffee or something?"

"I'd love some."

I put a tray together, including some of those sugar-free blueberry muffins I'd made for Sarah. My heart panged with regret. Would I end up throwing most of these away? Giving them to someone else? Freezing them?

The thought felt incredibly sad.

I pushed my feelings aside and brought the tray into the living room, setting it in front of Ms. Baldwin. She took the cup I offered her but turned down the baked goods.

"What's going on, Ms. Baldwin?" I started, lowering myself into the seat across from her.

"Please, call me Tam." She set her coffee mug down, her motions still jerky and uncertain. "And, again, I'm sorry to stop by without an invitation. I had to talk to you, though. Face-to-face."

"What's going on?" My concern increased. Did this have to do with Joe? Sarah? I had no clue at this point.

"I know it's weird that I was with Joe yesterday," she started.

"Your love life is none of my business." Though I had begun to question some of her judgment.

"I met Joe at the school a couple of weeks ago, and we went on a couple dates. He seems like a nice enough guy. Very charming."

"I bet." I still wasn't sure where Tam was going with this. But I hoped it was somewhere useful.

"I really don't think he would ever do anything to hurt any of the students."

"He was texting one of them," I reminded her.

"But it was only about a job opportunity." Tam's voice rose with emotion, and her words came out faster, stronger.

Her persistence didn't change my opinion, however. "A job opportunity that's potentially illegal, at worst. At best, it's questionable."

"He didn't realize that," she jumped in quickly again.

I licked my lips and tried to keep my tone gentle. "Why are you defending him, Tam?"

She shrugged. "I don't know. I just want to find Sarah. I haven't been able to stop thinking about her. But when I saw the police yesterday with Joe, I realized this really was serious. Much more serious than I would have ever guessed."

"We're still trying to piece together what's going on. Unfortunately, most of our leads have dried up."

"I'm sorry to hear that. I love teaching because I love the students. I still believe teachers have the power to change lives, you know."

"Yeah, I know. I think it's great that you found a job you love."

"I was at one of the nicer schools, but I transferred this year. I wanted to work with more at-risk kids because I felt like I had a bigger chance to influence them." She looked at her lap. "Anyway. I don't know why I'm telling you all of this. I just haven't been able to stop thinking about Sarah. I didn't sleep all night. Is there anything I can do?"

"Just pray. And if you get any leads at all—anything— let the police know."

She nodded. "I will. Thank you for letting me come over and interrupt your morning."

"It's not a problem, Tam."

CHAPTER 20

I SET aside thoughts of my conversation with Tam and turned them to Avril instead. Where had I seen that girl before? Her image still haunted me.

I went back to her social media page and scrolled through her photos and information again. There were plenty of pictures of her smiling with her friends with a school building in the background. A few of her sitting on her couch making goofy faces. The obligatory pictures taken in the bathroom mirror to showcase an outfit or new lipstick.

But I still had nothing to help me identify why she seemed familiar. Social work? Church? Youth center? There were so many possibilities.

"Where did our paths cross?" I muttered, staring at the picture.

Wait . . .

I sat up straight and navigated to a different page on my web browser. I sucked in a deep breath at what I saw.

Was this it? The link I'd been searching for? My gut said yes.

I scrolled through several pictures and, just to be certain, I paused. Using my mouse, I enlarged one of the photos and stared at it, allowing myself time to process.

There she was. Avril.

She sat in a chair and smiled as her peers looked at her with rapt attention. Her hands were raised, like she was telling an engaging story.

The photos were from a juvenile diabetes support group I'd attended twice with Sarah. Avril hadn't been there in person. No, she'd been missing by the time Sarah joined.

But I'd looked on this site, and I'd seen these promotional pictures before taking Sarah to attend for the first time.

Did Avril also have diabetes? And, if so, what did all of this mean?

"So you're thinking diabetes is the connection?" Chase questioned, leaning against his desk as I explained what I'd discovered.

I'd stopped by the police station and, thankfully, he'd been in his office. Otherwise, I would have tracked him down on the street . . . because I was just that kind of dedicated.

I shrugged at his question. "Maybe. Somehow. I'm not sure. I'm still wondering if maybe the diabetes test strips are the connection."

"I don't know, Holly." He shook his head and stared off into space for a moment. "It seems like a stretch."

Disappointment tried to bite at me, but I fought it off. "I know, but we don't have any more leads."

"I agree that we should explore it. Just don't get your hopes up."

I leaned closer, desperate for someone to see my point of view. "Chase, I also think you should look into the other foster kids who've gone missing. See if they have any connection to this."

"You really think they're connected with Sarah's disappearance?"

"I think . . . I think it's worth looking into. I'm not paid staff at Family Services anymore. They won't let me see those records, so I can't look for myself. Only you can."

"I'll see what I can do." He stood from behind his desk.

"Great." I stood also and glanced at my watch. "I'm going to go talk to the support group leader."

Chase gave me a look. "By yourself?"

"I can take Jamie with me if you'd like."

He leveled his gaze and pressed his lips together. "Listen, how about if I go with you?"

"I don't need a babysitter."

"I never said you did."

I crossed my arms, determined not to let him go if it was only out of obligation. "Don't you have other things to look into?"

"I do. I'll ask some of my colleagues to help out. I'll go with you."

I waited as Chase went to talk to someone else. A moment later, he returned, took my elbow, and led me toward the building's exit.

"By the way, did you ever find Sarah's mom?" I asked.

"No, we've tried to track her down, but it seems like she fell off the face of the earth. It's kind of strange."

"Then who was the woman in the photo?" The image hit my memory, and I pictured Sarah smiling beside the unknown woman.

"It's just another mystery we have to solve."

"I guess we do." There were just so many unanswered questions, though. So. Many.

I prayed the answers would be found soon.

CHAPTER 21

BRANDON GARRISON RAN the diabetic support group that met at an area hospital. The man seemed nice enough. I'd talked to him twice before when I brought Sarah to the meetings.

Brandon was a certified diabetes educator and a former nurse. I knew he had an office here at Grandview Medical, and I hoped to catch him. I didn't want to give him a heads-up I was coming. No, I wanted to catch him unaware and see his reaction with my own eyes when I asked about Sarah.

After being given directions by a volunteer at the front desk, I wound my way down the hall until I found a door with Brandon's name on it and knocked. I stepped inside before anyone responded.

Brandon stood from his desk when he saw me and straightened his jacket, crumbs from his lunch stuck to the front of his shirt and a glop of mayonnaise at the side of his lip.

"Hi, can I help you?" He wiped his shirt, suddenly looking self-conscious.

"Hi, Brandon. It's Holly. Holly Paladin. My foster daughter, Sarah, comes to your juvenile diabetes support group on Thursdays."

"Right. I remember the two of you." His gaze traveled to Chase.

"I'm Chase Dexter. Detective Chase Dexter." He extended his hand.

Brandon hesitated before taking it. "What can I do for the two of you?"

"We have a few questions for you," Chase said, using his professional voice. "Do you have a minute?"

Brandon glanced at his watch. "I have only a few more minutes of my lunch break before I have to go to a meeting. What do you need? Please, have a seat." He nodded to the chairs in front of him.

Chase and I lowered ourselves there. I was going to start—I had it all worked out in my head—but Chase jumped in before I did.

"Mr. Garrison, as you may be aware, Holly's foster daughter disappeared two days ago."

Brandon blinked again. "No, I hadn't heard. I'm really sorry to hear that, but I don't know what it has to do with me."

"As we were doing some research, we discovered another kid in the foster system disappeared several months earlier also," I added.

"Okay . . . I'm sorry. But I'm still not following." He picked up a canister of pencils on his desk but fumbled them, and they scattered over his desktop like an impromptu game of pickup sticks.

"That girl was also a part of this support group," Chase said.

Brandon swooped up the wreckage from his pencil jar and jammed them back inside. He turned back to us, obviously trying to compose himself. "That's . . . well, that's a terrible coincidence. Do you mind if I ask who the other person was?"

"A girl named Avril," I said, wondering why he seemed so nervous. Then again, I remembered him being rather clumsy at the meetings I'd attended.

He nodded. "Yes, I remember her. She was very active here. We even used her in some of our promotional materials."

"Usually foster kids aren't allowed to be photographed for things like that." How had he gotten around that?

"We took those pictures before she was in the foster care system," Brandon said. "In fact, Avril has been coming to these meetings for probably five years. She just went into the foster system maybe two years ago."

"I see." Chase shifted in his seat. "Did you have any other foster kids that you meet with?"

Brandon shrugged, otherwise remaining still—probably for fear of accidentally doing something else that would signal his guilt. "I can't say, really. I mean, I didn't do an interview with participants or anything. They just came with their guardians. Occasionally, someone would drop them off. But we didn't talk about the personal stuff as much as we talked about the disease and how to manage it."

I supposed that made sense.

Brandon shifted and looked at me, his nervousness replaced with concern. "Do you mind if I ask if Sarah took her medication with her?"

My spine clenched as I remembered all those details. "Long story short, we believe she has her medication."

"That's good, at least." He let out a breath, as if relieved. "I'm sure you know it could be a life-or-death situation otherwise."

"I'm aware."

"Anyway, I'm sorry to hear all of this, and I really wish there was more I could do."

"Mr. Garrison, is there anyone who comes to this

group who showed an unusual interest in Sarah?" Chase asked, his deep voice resonating in the small room.

Brandon straightened, some of the anxiety returning to his gaze again. "Wait. You think Sarah and Avril's disappearances are connected with this group?"

"We think it's a real possibility," Chase said. "This group is another link between them—that and foster care."

Brandon shook his head rapidly, and his hand flew out, nearly sending the pencil cannister toppling again. "Well, I have no idea. I run the group, and the kids come every month. Occasionally, we'll have a guest speaker."

"I'll need their names—the group members and the speakers," Chase said.

"Yes, of course. It will take me a few hours to collect everything."

"As soon as you can, please." Chase stood, and I followed his lead.

There was nothing else to ask. But I wondered if Chase and I were finally onto something.

Chase put his hand on my elbow as we left Brandon's office. Then he leaned close and whispered, "What do you think?"

"I think we're getting closer to answers. You?"

"I don't believe in coincidences. Two foster girls who've disappeared, both with diabetes and both who were a part of this group? Maybe someone else who participated in the group knows something."

"Or maybe someone else is the one who's involved with this," I said, sure to keep my voice low. "I think they meet again next week. I only wish next week didn't feel so far away."

"Ms. Paladin," someone called behind me.

I paused, Chase also, and turned to see Dr. Marks walking toward me, wearing his lab coat and carrying a clipboard in his hands. I was surprised he recognized me and remembered my name, but maybe he had one of those brains that worked like that.

"Hello, doctor," I said.

"I thought that was you." Mr. Marks paused and extended his hand toward Chase, introducing himself. Then he turned back to me. "Any updates on Sarah?"

I shook my head, wishing I had better news. "Unfortunately, no."

He nodded slowly, thoughtfully, but I could tell the news bothered him. "You've been on my mind, but I was hoping the outcome was different."

"The good news is that we believe Sarah has her diabetes medication now," I told him. "I think she has enough to last a week or so."

"You're right. I suppose that's good news." Dr. Marks pushed his glasses up on his nose, his eyes swaying as if processing something internally. "But I thought she disappeared without the medication?"

I shifted. The man had a good memory. "We believe she came back to get them."

The doctor shifted, his gaze fixated on the wall behind us for a moment as he seemed to analyze my words. "So you think she left on her own accord?"

I wasn't ready to buy into that theory yet. Not completely, at least. "Though that's how it seems, I still believe she could have been coerced. The details are still uncertain."

He let out a soft grunt that indicated he was listening and thinking still. "I see."

While I had him here, maybe he could clear up a couple of questions I had. It couldn't hurt to try, at least. "Doctor, if you have a minute, I'm concerned that maybe someone took Sarah's medication to sell it. Do you have any information or experience about people who sell diabetes medication and supplies for profit?"

He pushed his gold-rimmed glasses up higher again. "I have seen those signs around town, and I have a limited knowledge of the practice, if that's what you would call it. As you know, some people believe we have a health-care crisis in this country. Some medications are outrageously priced, which prevents people who need those medications from getting them. It's really a shame."

"I can understand where they're coming from," I said, trying to steer clear of any debates on the topic.

"But without getting into those logistics, I do know that people have taken to buying prescriptions overseas to save money," Dr. Marks continued. "The problem is that these supplies are not always the highest quality, nor did they pass the same standards that US-approved medications do."

"Right." I'd pretty much read that online.

His jaw flexed, and he stared off in silent thought again. "I suppose it would be possible that someone could be desperate for some of those medications as well as the test strips. They could either be desperate to get some for themselves or to sell them to other people who are desperate."

"That's what I'm afraid of." Had Sarah set out on her own and sold the only items in her possession that were worth anything?

But there were other things she could have taken from my place if it had been out of desperation for cash. I had a limited amount of jewelry. Some crystal dishes. It wasn't much, but it would have brought in some profit for her.

This whole thing just didn't make sense.

"Unfortunately, there are thirty million people in this

country with diabetes," Dr. Marks continued. "And selling test strips isn't illegal. I suppose the police could investigate more, but they have bigger fish to fry—like the opioid epidemic."

"That's a huge issue in the country right now," Chase said.

"The problem is that these underground supplies aren't always as accurate," Dr. Marks said. "These people don't know what they're getting. They don't know if the strips are expired or if they've been tampered with. These people are really taking their lives into their own hands by depending on them."

"That's what I suspected also," I said.

"I strongly caution my patients to steer clear. I try to find grants for them whenever I can. I understand how costly sickness can be, but I don't feel finances should ever be a reason for people to not receive the help they deserve."

"I agree." I wished there were more doctors out there like Dr. Marks—doctors who truly cared for their patients.

Dr. Marks shrugged. "I don't know what else to say. I wish I could be of more help. If you find her—when you find her, I mean—I'm here. She'll need to be seen, I imagine. Thankfully she's old enough to manage the insulin pump on her own . . . at least until her refills run out."

"You've been a big help," I said. "That's what I needed to know. And I'll definitely be in touch."

Because I was going to find Sarah, if it was the last thing I did.

CHAPTER 22

BACK IN CHASE'S CAR, he gave me an update. I'd seen him on his phone once and texting a couple times while I'd been talking to the doctor, so I figured there was a new development.

"Detective Colerain called the Family Services office, and they do have records of one more of the missing children having diabetes."

My pulse spiked. "Is that right?"

"Colerain is looking into this teen right now." Chase cranked the engine and pulled out of the lot.

"Did he tell you anything about him or her?"

"It's a him. Sixteen. Disappeared two years ago. Name was George."

"Let me guess—the foster parents thought he just ran away?"

"That seems to be the story." Chase frowned. "Colerain also talked to someone on the other end of one of the diabetic test strip ads."

"And?" Had it been the same person I called? Did this guy actually call Colerain back? I was slightly offended.

"And this guy wants to meet with him, but he's not available until tomorrow. Colerain tried to press him to meet sooner, but it didn't work."

"Maybe it's a lead."

"Maybe it is. It's hard to say at this point. It's like we inch closer only to be thrown back by a mile."

"Exactly!" I ran a hand over my face. "Do you think this Brandon guy is somehow involved? Maybe he's giving someone leads as to which kids have diabetes so they can target them?"

"I'll look into his background. It's an idea worth exploring. I didn't get that feeling from him, though." He paused. "I'm also going to talk to Avril's foster parents and see if I can find out anything from them. I don't have high hopes—especially considering the fact that I hadn't even heard of her disappearance until now."

Did someone else realize that? Was the bad guy here preying on the fact that foster kids were, in some ways, alone in the world? That most people would assume they left on their own? My grief felt heavier at the thought.

Chase stopped in front of my house and hesitated a moment.

Finally, I put my hand on the door handle, an unseen weight pressing on me. "Thanks for everything, Chase."

"Anytime, Holly. Stay safe. And call me if you need me."

"I will." And that was my problem, I realized. When I needed someone, Chase was not the number I should dial. Yet that's all I seemed to be doing lately.

An hour later, I sat in Jamie's bedroom. She still lived at home with her parents and her five brothers, and most of the time she seemed pretty content with it.

Where my family was stiff and conservative, her family was loud and gregarious, and I loved coming over here for the change of pace. Here, I never had to wonder what someone was thinking. Nope, her family told you— even when you didn't want to know.

Her three youngest brothers, adopted from Haiti, were full of life and messy. Jamie's father, a musician, was constantly practicing an instrument for an upcoming church service or concert or lesson. Her mom could preach a hell-fire and brimstone sermon in thirty seconds flat, including an altar call. It was amazing.

It was craziness.

But I still liked it.

Just like we used to do when we were in college,

Jamie and I lay on our backs across her bed and let our heads hang over the edge, our hair stretching down below us.

We used to call this our thinking pose.

I gave Jamie an update on everything. A lot had happened since we last talked.

"It sounds like there are a lot of possibilities as to what happened to Sarah," Jamie said. "But that message you got on Chatbook? It's strange. You really think Sarah sent it?"

I shrugged. "I don't really know. My gut tells me no. But then when you throw in the missing medicine and medical supplies . . . maybe the pieces do fit together, but maybe I'm only seeing what I want to see. Maybe Sarah's first instinct was to run and to fend for herself, and I'm refusing to acknowledge it."

"I didn't get that sense about her, either."

I glanced at Jamie. "You didn't?"

"No, I think she was looking for a safe place. I really thought she'd found that with you."

"Me too." It was so good to talk to someone who could see eye to eye with me, even when we were on our backs staring at a scuffed-up lilac wall and a line of shoes against it. If Jamie let me, I could do amazing things to her room—things like organize it.

"Tell me what it's been like working with Chase."

I let out a long breath, remembering the drama of the

past couple of days. "He apparently thinks I abandoned him."

"What?" Jamie's voice screeched higher. "You're kidding."

"No, he laid it all on the line. He feels like I walked away and left him standing alone. And he thinks I'll be miserable with Drew." My heart still hurt as I replayed the conversation.

"Well, of course, he's going to think that." She let out a snort. "What brought that on?"

"I helped Drew out at the funeral home yesterday."

"Oh." Her voice dropped.

"Why did you say it like that?" I glanced over at her in confusion. There was more to that "oh" than Jamie showing me she was listening.

"I said it like that because you never seem like yourself after you go to that funeral home."

"It's a solemn place. It's supposed to change you."

"But is it supposed to depress you?"

"Depress me? You think I'm depressed?"

"Not deeply depressed. But you definitely seem melancholy whenever you go there. I really hope Drew doesn't expect you to help him there if you guys get married."

I sat up, needing to look at Jamie for the rest of this conversation. She followed my lead until we sat cross-legged in front of each other.

"You've noticed I act miserable there too, huh? I've just been trying to be the bigger person. To push aside my own preferences and do what's best for Drew and me as a couple."

Jamie did her signature Z snap—a move she used whenever she needed to drive home a point. "Girl, this is the rest of your life you're talking about. If you're prepared to live this way for the rest of your life, then go for it."

I studied her face, trying to read her expression. "But you don't think I should."

She shrugged. "It's your choice. I can't make it for you, and if I give you bad advice, you'll spend the rest of your life resenting me."

"I wouldn't do that." She had to know me better than that.

"Not on a conscious level, but on an unconscious level. I'm just saying I'd think long and hard about it before committing to forever. I like Drew. I like him a lot. I like the way he treats you and practically worships the ground you walk on."

"But?" I held my breath.

"But I think Chase challenged you. He brought out a fire in you. He pushed you outside of your idealistic, perfectly mannered ways."

"So you're saying?" I really needed her to spell things out for me here.

Her head dropped to the side. "I'm saying you should choose wisely. And I wouldn't want to be in your shoes."

I rubbed my temples. "I don't want to be in my shoes."

She chuckled. "It's too late for that. But at least those shoes are cute."

CHAPTER 23

I ATE DINNER WITH JAMIE—HER mother's famous Slap Your Mama It's So Good Jambalaya—and then I headed home. Just as I got back to my house, my head loaded with questions, I spotted Tam Baldwin sitting on my porch.

Another visit? Surprise coursed through me.

She stood from the steps when she spotted me, but her back was hunched with an invisible weight. She wrung her hands together, and her eyes were red-rimmed still.

"Holly, I'm sorry to show up like this again, but I need to talk to you."

"What's going on?" I paused on the sidewalk in front of her.

She stepped down to join me, her face lined with

grimness. "I can't stop thinking about Sarah and everything that's going on. I called Joe and I asked him if I could come over."

"Today?" She couldn't have been home from school for too long.

"I took a sick day, and Joe only works three days a week. It's not a full-time job. Anyway, I tried to make it sound like it was because I was interested in him. Anyway, he said okay and made some joke about how he didn't think I'd ever want to see him again after yesterday."

"Go on." I really needed her to get to the point before I passed out from exhaustion.

She raked a hand through her hair. "So I went to his apartment. I asked him to go pick up some Chinese food for lunch and while he was gone, I started to snoop around. I know I probably shouldn't have done it, but . . . I don't know. I kept thinking about how he'd been texting Sarah with that job opportunity. It just seems so not cool, you know."

My heart rate spiked. "Did you find anything?"

"Not at first. But then I realized he'd left his phone at the apartment."

Maybe we were finally getting somewhere. "Could you get on it?"

Tam nodded, but her eyes were still wide and nervous, making her look a touch like a bobblehead doll. "Yeah, I knew his code. I saw him type it in once and . . . well, I'm just nosy."

A woman after my own heart. "What did you find, Tam?"

"Initially? Nothing. But then I discovered he had this secret app where you can hide things. I only know about it because there was a presentation for parents at school about what to look out for pertaining to students on social media. This app was mentioned there. It looks like a calculator."

"Okay, so there was an app with hidden things. What kind of hidden things?" Was this the lead we were looking for? I could hardly wait any longer to hear the rest.

Tam's face scrunched together with pain and disgust and anxiety—a mishmash of negative emotions that seemed to capture and overtake her features. "There are pictures there, Holly. Pictures of girls. They look like they're high school age."

My heart rate spiked simultaneous to the dread that pooled in my stomach. "You think he's been stalking students at the school?"

"I have no idea. But it was creepy. The photos were the kind taken when no one was looking, you know?"

"Was Sarah in any of those photos?" I didn't want to ask the question, but I had to. I had to know, whether I wanted to or not.

"Sarah was in one. It looked like it had been taken while she was in school. She was sitting outside on the curb eating lunch." Tam's face crumbled as a sob escaped. "What should I do, Holly?"

"Let me call the detective on the case. He'll know what to do. Can he call you if he has any questions?"

"Of course." She nodded and handed me something from the pocket of her jeans. "I took Joe's phone. I know I shouldn't have. But I did. I ran before he got back."

That meant this evidence would never hold up in a court of law. But I'd let Chase deal with that. "Do you have somewhere to lie low, just in case he comes looking for you?"

"I'm going to go to one of my friend's houses."

"Do that. And be alert. If you need help, call the police. Don't take any chances."

"I will."

I held up the phone. "Thanks, Tam. I appreciate you letting me know about this."

"I just hope it's not too late."

I paced my living room floor, anxiously awaiting the outcome of the whole Joe Richardson saga. I'd called Chase, and he'd stopped by to get the phone. After he saw the photos, he told me he was sending a team over to Joe's place to question him again.

He'd also told me that I couldn't go along this time, but he'd promised to update me.

That had been three hours ago.

Which meant that I'd been pacing now for 180 minutes.

I'd downed several cups of coffee, trying to keep myself alert. But I'd been tempted just to crawl in bed and take a quick power nap. I didn't. I feared I would miss something. Maybe Joe really was behind this.

Finally, Chase pulled up. I saw his car out front—yes, I'd been watching for it.

I opened the door before he even reached the front steps and stared at him a moment, waiting for him to fill me in.

"Joe did take those pictures," Chase started, stepping past me and inside my house. I followed and shut the door. "There were no incriminating photos that indicated he'd done anything wrong. Is he a creep? Yes. Does he need to be working in the school system? No. But can we pin Sarah's disappearance on him? No."

"So you just let him go?" I practically screeched. This had seemed like the real thing—like the answers were so close.

"No, I didn't just let him go. We have an officer who's watching him. But there's nothing in Joe's financial records or background that would indicate he's involved in Sarah's disappearance."

"I bet the same can be said of a lot of criminals."

"If Joe took Sarah, there's no indication as to where he might have taken her. There's not enough evidence to arrest him. So all we can do is watch and wait. I know that's not what you want to hear."

"I just want answers." I heard the exhaustion and resignation in my voice as clear as day.

"That's what we're trying to find. We also have someone watching Cameron, and we have another officer who's exploring the lead you gave us about the missing foster kids. We're doing everything we can, Holly, even if it doesn't seem like it."

I released my breath and folded my shoulders in. "I know you are. I'm sorry. I just keep praying that we'll have some resolution on this. That we'll have answers. And we don't. Every lead is a dead end."

"Not having answers is hard." Chase's gaze felt electric on mine, like it was something I could reach out and touch.

I looked away. "I'm sure you know that better than most people."

He offered a curt nod, and that was all he needed to say. Of course, he understood.

"So where does that leave us?" I asked. "I mean, where does it leave *you*?"

He smiled. "I don't mind that you're helping, Holly. But I can only let you go so far."

"I realize that. I don't want to get in your way. I really don't." I remembered what Bishop had said. Chase might never admit that, but it felt good to know that my opinion and help was valued—even if it was *discreetly* valued.

"It leaves us with the footwork part of this investigation," Chase said. "We're not making quick progress. I know that. But we haven't given up. We have a lot of balls in the air. A lot of possibilities."

"A lot of possible dead ends is more like it."

"Or maybe not," Chase said.

I turned away, putting space between the two of us.

"There's another reason I came by," Chase said. "The diabetic test strip guy called. His schedule changed, and he has an opening for today. In an hour, actually."

Finally, some good news. "Who's going?"

"I am."

"Let me come with you. After all, he's going to see you're a cop a mile away. Let me talk to him."

"It's too dangerous, Holly."

"What if I go with you then? We can pose as boyfriend/girlfriend. It will make you seem less auspicious."

He drew his head back as if offended. "You think I'm that bad of an actor?"

"Yes," I said the answer without too much thought before softening my tone. "I mean, you're big and intimidating. And I'm . . ." How did I say it?

"Warm and cuddly?"

I shrugged. Maybe not the exact words I was looking for. "Something like that. Most people aren't intimidated by me. They'd rather eat one of my cookies and get a hug."

Chase let out a sigh. "Fine. You can come. And you can talk. But you have to promise to listen to me."

"Of course."

Once I was inside Chase's car, he handed me a bag.

"Here are some test strips," he said.

I peeked inside, saw the boxes, and nodded. "You thought of everything."

He shrugged. "Not quite. But coming empty-handed would be the first sign we were up to something."

I nodded and gathered myself up tall. "Okay. I'm ready when you are."

We left to meet the man and parked in a lot two blocks away from the meeting location, just so the unmarked sedan didn't raise any suspicions. We were in a part of town close to the UC—the University of Cincinnati.

We walked to the corner where the man had said to meet. A deli stood behind us, and even though the sky was just beginning to darken, numerous college students with backpacks hurried past. A fair number of skateboarders and businessmen also cluttered the sidewalk.

If the man buying these supplies had wanted a public meeting spot, he'd found it here.

My gaze cut through the crowd until I spotted our guy.

Skippy Lebowski was waiting for us, leaning against the side of a brick building, with one foot propped up behind him and a cigarette in his mouth. He straightened when he saw us, seeming to sense we were his contacts.

"Hey, I'm Skippy. You here about the test strips?" Gone was his streetwise look. When he spoke, his voice sounded surprisingly smooth, and his dialogue almost had a professional vibe to it.

"We are," I said, looping my arm through Chase's. I ignored the realization that the action felt entirely too natural. "I heard you want to buy some."

"That's right. We're trying to help people who can't afford them by offering other options."

"I know they're expensive." I kept my voice calm and even. "Thankfully, insurance provides them for us. We have more than we need."

The man's gaze shifted back and forth from me to Chase. "One of you diabetic?"

187

I shook my head. "No, but our daughter, Ella, is. She's ten."

Ella? The name had slipped out. But it was what I planned on naming my daughter one day.

"I'm sorry to hear that. It's a tough disease."

"She's doing okay, however. We're grateful for that." As I said the words, a sweep of lightheadedness hit me, and I felt myself wobble for a minute.

Was it my lack of sleep? Had I eaten today? Maybe those things along with stress were starting to take their toll on me.

Chase seemed to sense it and grabbed my elbow to steady me.

"So, look, I usually pay twenty dollars for a box." Skippy jerked his shoulder up in a quick shrug. "I know it seems low, but it will give you some extra pocket change and help out my customers."

"How much do you sell it to them for?" Chase asked.

Skippy's jaw tightened, as if he didn't appreciate the question. "Fifty."

Anger surged through me at the outrageous difference. "Why the steep markup? I thought you were trying to help."

"It's still a bargain, especially for people who need them." Defiance flared to life in Skippy's eyes.

I stepped closer. "Are you sure you're not just preying on desperate people?"

His eyes darkened. "I'm sure. Look, if you're not comfortable with this, there's no pressure. But I do run a business. It's fair that I make something from this."

"I think we're more comfortable finding people who need these and just giving them away," Chase said, inserting himself into the conversation. "I'll sleep better at night doing it that way."

Skippy's eyes turned icy cold. "If that's what you want to do. But I have customers who could really use them. You're right. They are desperate. If they don't get some strips, it could put them in a life-or-death situation."

"Then you should do the right thing and not upcharge them so much," I told him.

He raised a hand in a stop signal. "I can see the conversation is finished. Have a good day."

"Wait!" I called. I couldn't let him leave here before we had any answers.

Skippy paused, but I could tell he wouldn't stay long. I only had a few seconds to make my case.

"Did this girl try to sell you anything?" I held up Sarah's picture on my phone.

His eyes narrowed as he looked at the picture. "I've never seen her."

"Look more closely. Are you sure? This is important."

He scowled this time and shook his head. "I'm sure."

"She needs help. We need to find her." Desperation stained my voice. I could hear it.

Skippy's scowl deepened. "Look, lady. I don't know what kind of game you're playing, but I don't know her. Now I'm out of here."

He walked away.

As he did, I saw an undercover cop follow him. That was the plan.

The plainclothes officer would tail him. See if Sarah was at his place. See if there was any reason to question Skippy further.

Chase's hand went to my elbow. But before he could say anything, we both jerked our attention toward shouting taking place only a few feet away.

A homeless man was heckling a woman who passed, trying to get money. She snipped back at him, and now the two were coming to blows with each other.

"Excuse me a minute," Chase muttered. He stepped toward the argument, ready to intercede.

As he did, another wave of dizziness hit me.

I reached for something—anything—to grab. But before my hand could connect with the street sign beside me, my gaze went to a car traveling down the street.

Only it was traveling too fast.

And headed toward me.

Before I could jump out of the way, I heard Chase yell my name.

Then everything went black.

CHAPTER 24

I OPENED my eyes and saw Chase beside me. His eyes brightened when he saw me stirring. "Holly. You're awake."

"What . . .?" I blinked, unsure where I was or how I'd gotten here or what had happened.

I glanced around. Was I at . . . the hospital?

Looking down, I saw a hospital gown covering me. An IV was connected to my arm. A heart monitor connected to the skin on my chest.

"You passed out," Chase explained, gripping my hand. "And nearly got hit by a car."

"What?" I remembered meeting with Skippy. Chase going to intercede during that fight with the homeless man. Seeing that car coming my way.

And then nothing.

Until now.

"You've been admitted overnight for observation. I called your mom, but she's at a meeting an hour away in Kentucky," Chase continued. "She's on her way now."

An hour away? I pushed myself up higher in my hospital bed, noting how my entire body ached. "How long have I been here?"

"You passed out over an hour ago. The doctor also gave you a sedative and ran some tests on you in the interim," Chase continued. "Maybe he'll know something soon so you can have some answers."

My heart rate quickened. I didn't like the sound of that. "Tests? What kind of tests?"

Memories rushed back to me. Memories of when I'd been misdiagnosed with a life-ending disease and given only months to live. I remembered *those* tests well. That time in the hospital. Of having my future turned upside down.

Later, I'd been told the diagnosis was incorrect. But, in the back of my mind, the doubt lingered that maybe the doctor was wrong again. Once a person received a diagnosis like that, you were a changed person and you never went back. You never forgot.

And though I trusted God with my future and I knew my days here on earth were numbered—everyone's were —that still didn't make death an easy pill to swallow, even for the most graceful of souls.

"Just blood tests," Chase said.

I cleared my throat, determined to flee from those thoughts before they prematurely made me a corpse. "Did you find the driver who almost hit me?"

"No. I was distracted—too worried about you. But another officer is working on it."

"How about the officer following Skippy? Anything?"

Chase let out a faint chuckle and shook his head. "You're a very focused woman, Holly Anna. And, no, we don't know anything yet. You should probably turn that focus now on feeling better."

"But . . ." I paused and shook my head. I didn't even know what to say—other than that thinking about this mystery was easier than thinking about my health problems.

"Holly . . ." Chase's voice sounded hoarse and his eyes were watery as he gripped my hand.

"Yes?" I could tell he wanted to say something important—and something that was hard for him. I braced myself for whatever that might be.

His fingers rubbed against mine. "I . . . I just need to tell you—"

Before he could finish, the door flew open, and Drew rushed inside.

My heart plummeted. What was Chase about to say?

Chase quickly pulled his hand back and stood, all

signs of his earlier emotions being erased as I looked at him.

If Drew noticed, he didn't acknowledge it. He rushed to my bedside and kissed my forehead. "I just heard. Are you okay? What happened?"

The questions hit me like ammunition from a machine gun. "I don't know much. I . . . I just woke up."

Drew turned to Chase, his nostrils flaring. "Did you do this?"

Chase straightened. "Me? What do you mean? How could I have done this?"

"You shouldn't let her participate in your investigations. You should tell her no. She's not a trained officer of the law."

Chase's face went rigid along with the rest of his body. "Have you ever tried to stop her?"

"That's your job," Drew said, staring Chase down.

I held my breath, not wanting this whole confrontation to happen. I had other things to worry about. Like feeling better. Finding Sarah.

"I do my job, and I do it well," Chase said. "Maybe you should stick to doing your job and leave Holly out of your line of work as well. Can't you see the toll it takes on her?"

"What does that even mean?" Drew's voice climbed higher. "I work at a funeral home. What's so dangerous about that?"

"Guys!" I called, my voice sounding feeble against their adrenaline-laced words. "Please stop. Not now."

Both of them stared each other down one more moment before turning away and at least trying to look more relaxed.

"I'm sorry, Holly." Drew turned toward me, his anger disappearing. "You're my first concern, of course."

"I'm going to go." Chase nodded toward the door. "I'll check in later."

Before I could even say goodbye or thank you, Chase left. I watched as he disappeared, taking one last glance back at me.

What did I even say now? I wanted to fuss at Drew, but did I even have the right to do that? I didn't know. And my head hurt.

"How did you hear I was here?" I asked instead.

"Chase called me." Drew's words sounded stiff.

"That was . . . nice of him."

Drew scowled before drawing in a deep breath and attempting a comforting smile. "Did the doctor say anything?"

I shook my head, recalling the update I'd gotten from Chase, which hadn't told me much. "I just woke up. Apparently, doctors did some tests on me."

Drew's jaw clenched. "We need to find the doctor and figure out what's going on."

Before we could do that, my family burst in through the door.

I was thankful when the doctor shooed everyone out of the room an hour later. Darkness had fallen outside now, and the clock on the wall told me it was 10:00 p.m.

What a day.

At least maybe I could clear my head for a minute. But when I saw the look in Dr. Harris's eyes, some of the relief vanished.

He glanced at the electronic tablet in his hands. "I saw in your charts that you were misdiagnosed with subcutaneous panniculitis-like T-cell lymphoma a couple of years ago."

"That's correct." My throat burned as I said the words. Just hearing the name of the disease said aloud caused terrible memories to batter my psyche.

Dr. Harris frowned and kept staring at something on his screen. "Holly, I'd like to do some more tests on you."

"I'm fine," I said, desperation causing my voice to catch. "I just haven't been taking care of myself the way I should lately. I've been under a lot of stress, and it's affected my eating and sleeping habits. I'll do better."

"I understand that, but a few markers in your blood

tests came back elevated. I want to be certain that there's nothing more going on, just to be on the safe side."

I wanted to argue, but I knew it was useless. If something was wrong with me, I needed to know. I couldn't live in denial . . . but it was tempting. So tempting.

"How long will I be here? My foster daughter is missing, and I need to find her." I didn't have time for any of this.

"Let me keep you overnight, okay?"

I opened my mouth to say no but stopped myself. "Okay. Can you just let my family know I need to rest and that I'll call them later?"

"I think some rest sounds like a good idea. We'll give you another sedative to help you rest. In the meantime, I'll let everyone outside know you need to sleep."

I closed my eyes, trying to shut out worst-case scenarios. Scenarios with new diagnoses. Old diagnoses. Life-changing news that turned everything a person thought they knew upside down. News that made today's problems seem inconsequential—well, today's problems minus Sarah.

I tried to ignore my worries, but they danced in my head, taunting me.

Do not worry about tomorrow because no one knows what tomorrow will bring.

I repeated the Bible verse over and over.

But the worry kept creeping in anyway until my head pounded.

Finally, I felt myself drifting between worlds. One minute, I was with Sarah again. At my house. Making sugar-free muffins with almond flour. The next minute, I could hear the beat of the heart monitor beside me. My eyelids felt heavy, and everything was blurry around me.

Then I was back with Sarah. Except she was no longer smiling. No, she was yelling. Throwing things. And then she ran away.

A shadowy figure waited outside my house for her, and they disappeared together. I yelled after her, but she didn't even bother to turn back.

Then I heard the heart monitor again.

Movement crackled the stillness of my room. Who had come in? My mom? Drew? Maybe a nurse?

Everything was so fuzzy, and the line between dreams and reality blurred.

I tried to open my eyes, but I couldn't. They were too heavy, almost weighted. Even when I managed to lift them just barely a slit, everything was fuzzy.

"You should have stayed out of it," someone whispered.

My entire body—every muscle—tensed.

Was I awake? Or asleep? Or . . . I didn't know. I tried again to open my eyes but couldn't.

"You're going to ruin everything. Do you hear me?"

I wasn't sure what I was hearing. Or who was talking. Was this a dream?

Why did it feel so real?

Because it was.

Open your eyes, Holly. See who's in the room with you.

But my body didn't cooperate. Had someone given me more drugs? Was I having an episode? I didn't know.

Scream. Just scream.

I tried to open my mouth. But I couldn't do that either. All I could do was lie there, helpless.

"This is your last warning. If you don't stay out of it, there will be dire consequences. Just let Sarah go."

And then I felt a pain like I'd never felt racing down my arm and through my body.

CHAPTER 25

EVERYTHING WAS A BLUR. Nurses had rushed into my room. Then doctors. Reality felt dreamlike around me.

Finally, some of the haze around me faded, and life came into focus. Dr. Harris stood over me. "You had an episode."

I squeezed my eyes shut, my pulse still racing with panic. "What kind of episode?"

"We're not sure. Your heart rate spiked dangerously high, but we can't figure out why."

I remembered the voice. *This is your last warning. If you don't stay out of it, there will be dire consequences. Just let Sarah go.* "Someone was in here with me. They did something to me. Did you check my IV? Did they put something into it?"

"We're checking your bloodwork and vitals, but no one was in here with you, Ms. Paladin."

I closed my eyes again, feeling a strange emptiness inside me at his words. "You're wrong."

"We're going to take you back for a CAT scan before we discharge you later today," he finally said. "Maybe that will offer some answers."

I could tell by the way the doctor looked at me that he felt sorry for me. That he thought I was delusional.

But I wasn't.

Yet I had nothing to prove what had happened—only blurry dreams and a memory of total panic.

He finally left, and, several minutes later, my mom and Drew came in. I glanced at the time. Six a.m. Had that much time really passed?

I could read their expressions also, and I could tell they thought something was wrong with me. Not physically wrong, mind you. Mentally wrong.

I stared at them as they stood by my bed, and I licked my dry lips as I chose my words. "I'm not losing it."

"We never said that you were," my mom said.

I frowned, wishing she wouldn't skirt around the truth with me. "You don't have to say it. It's written on your faces."

"You were medicated, Holly," Drew said quietly. "Maybe whatever they have you on was just messing with your brain."

I shook my head, causing the room to wobble for a minute until I closed my eyes and everything righted itself.

"It wasn't medication," I said, my teeth nearly clenched. "Someone came in this room and threatened me. And he did something to me. To my arm."

I reached for my bicep, expecting to feel a cut. But there was nothing, only tenderness and bad memories.

Mom frowned with worry. "The doctors couldn't find anything, Holly. Maybe this . . ."

I knew what she was going to say. Maybe this was some kind of new symptom of cancer. Maybe it had spread. Maybe the disease was in my brain.

Wouldn't the doctors know that by now? I honestly didn't know.

But I did know that I wasn't losing my mind.

"What happened last night was real." No one was going to convince me otherwise. I would believe it all the way to my deathbed—which, unfortunately, might be closer than I would like.

Drew could pick out a lovely casket for me, and my mom would design the best funeral ever with her planning and organizing skills.

I frowned at the thought. Why was I thinking like this? I had to stop.

Mom and Drew exchanged a glance with each other, a loaded glance that showed in its entirety what they were thinking: that I might be losing my mind.

"I want to be alone," I muttered, pulling my covers up higher. "I'm exhausted."

"I'm not sure that's a good idea," Drew said.

"If nothing happened, and it was all in my mind, then I don't see what the big deal is." My words had an unfortunate bitter edge to them.

They exchanged another look. But my compassion had waned. I needed someone to believe me. Instead, I felt like they were forming a club for people who thought I was incapable.

Before either of them could convince me to listen to them, I turned over in the bed, ready to get some rest. A moment later, I felt someone kiss me on the forehead. Drew, I thought. Someone else squeezed my arm. Probably my mom.

Then I heard footsteps. A door open. A door shut. And quiet.

As soon as I was sure they were gone, I turned back over, picked up the phone at my bedside, and I called Chase. Maybe *he* would take me seriously.

"Holly?" He sounded confused or like I'd just woken him. It *was* only seven a.m.

"Chase, I need you . . . to come to the hospital."

He paused. "I'm not sure if that's a good idea. I don't think I'm welcome, Holly. Drew made that clear."

I remembered that painful conversation—one I'd had no part of. I wasn't in the mood to walk on eggshells right now. "It's just me. I sent everyone home."

He still seemed to hesitate. "What's going on?"

"I'll explain when you get here. But it's important. I promise it is. And no one else believes me. You're the only one I can talk to about this."

He remained quiet a moment then finally said, "Okay, I'll be right there."

Thirty minutes later, Chase stood beside my bed, a cup of coffee in his hand for himself and another cup—for me—on my hospital tray.

I hadn't enjoyed it yet. No, my stomach was churning with unease. The IV in my arm hurt, and my exhaustion was catching up with me.

Chase didn't look much better, though he had showered, based on his damp hair. I'd guess he'd been up most of the night again.

"So you think someone came into your room in the middle of the night and threatened you?" Chase repeated. He didn't look quite as disbelieving as everyone else had.

I nodded, my memories fuzzy yet clear at the same time. "Yes, that's exactly what I think."

"And you said this man hurt you in some way?"

"It was a pain unlike anything I've felt before. It started in my arm and spread through my entire body. I don't even know how to describe it."

Chase frowned, worry creasing his brow. "The doctor checked you out?"

"And he didn't find anything. Maybe he just thinks I'm mental."

"Where did the pain start?"

"In my arm." I pointed to my bicep area.

Chase lifted my arm, and I tried not to jerk at his touch. But the jolt I felt when his skin connected with mine was unmistakable.

His finger traced down my skin as he examined it. I had to look away, to close my eyes before I revealed too much of my heart. No, I needed to keep these pieces of me to myself.

A true lady honors her commitments. She stands by the ones she loves. She's not tossed to and from by the currents of emotion and impulse.

It was advice from one of the etiquette books I liked to refer to. Most would say it was outdated and antiquated. But I still liked it and thought the words held truth.

"Look at that." Chase leaned closer and squinted at my arm.

"What is it?" I had no idea what he might be referring to, but his tone caused a shiver to race down my spine.

He squinted still. "I can't be sure. But I think it's . . . it's the marks from a stun gun."

I sucked in a quick breath. "Really?"

"That's my best guess. And your symptoms would match how it feels when someone uses one on you."

His theory made sense. Someone had sneaked into my hospital room, threatened me, and then used a Taser. It would explain my elevated heartrate and the fact that there were no other symptoms the doctor could find.

But there was still one thing that didn't make sense. "Why would someone do that, Chase?"

He straightened and ran a hand over his face. "You're obviously making someone feel threatened, Holly. Desperate people do desperate things."

I didn't know whether to be comforted or more fearful. "Who would have gotten in here? The hospital is closed at night. Wouldn't the nurses have seen something?"

"I suppose anyone could have slipped inside. We didn't have a guard stationed outside your room or anything."

My mind raced through people who would have access to the hospital during the night hours. Hospital staff. Police. Other patients. "What about the diabetes group coordinator—Brandon Garrison? He could have been here."

Chase cocked an eyebrow. "You really think he's a suspect?"

"I don't know." I honestly didn't. "But he has an office here, and he did have contact with two of the kids who are missing. Maybe our suspect has been in front of us this whole time."

"Three kids with diabetes have disappeared from the area's foster-care system within the past two years. I don't like that statistic."

"I don't either." I knew that Hamilton County, where Cincinnati was located, had approximately one thousand kids in the system. I also knew that approximately .024 percent of youth under the age of twenty had diabetes. That meant that only about twenty-four kids in the county system had some form of diabetes.

Chase let out a breath and stared off into the distance for a moment. Then, he righted himself and stepped toward the door.

"What are you doing?"

"I'm going to check out the security camera footage for this hallway." He paused and turned back toward me. "And I'm sorry that you're going through all of this, Holly."

"It wasn't your fault, no matter what Drew says." That conversation, every time I thought of it, felt like a punch in the gut. How could Drew have blamed Chase?

Chase didn't acknowledge that my words were true.

Instead, he said, "I'm not going to let anything happen to you."

A smile flickered across my face. "I know, Chase."

He paused. Stared at me. Looked like he wanted to say more.

Then nodded. "I'll be back."

CHAPTER 26

CHASE RETURNED to my room three hours later. I saw him peek inside to check to see if I was awake before stepping in and closing the door. Of course I was awake. I'd come back from my CAT scan, and I hadn't been able to rest.

I'd demanded the doctor take my IV out. I didn't want any kind of medication being fed into me. Not after what had happened last night.

Everyone else might think I was crazy. But I knew I wasn't.

Chase pulled up a chair beside my bed and sat there. He looked tired, and even his black T-shirt and jeans looked rumpled. He was obviously working too hard again. When was the last time he had slept?

"Hey, did you find out anything?" I asked.

"Unfortunately, the camera cuts off before reaching your room, so I wasn't able to see who came inside. I *was* able to see everyone who came off the elevator and who walked past the nurses' station, however."

"Anyone familiar?"

He exhaled. "Brandon Garrison, the diabetes educator, did come up this way around 3:00 a.m. I just sent someone to check him out. I haven't heard back yet."

"Okay . . ." I felt like Chase had more to say.

"I also thought it was interesting that Joe Richardson was here last night."

I sucked in a quick breath. "Joe, the school fundraiser guy?"

"He's the one."

"Why would he be here?" My mind raced through possibilities but came up with nothing.

"Since I wasn't far from his apartment, I went to talk to him before coming back here."

"And?" Had Joe done this to me? Did he know that Tam had told me about those photos, and had he tried to exact revenge?

Chase frowned. "And he said he hurt his ankle while he was working out at the gym last night."

My lungs deflated, along with my hope. "Did hospital records verify his story?"

"They seemed to. I don't think an injury like that would be hard to fake, however. Joe didn't break anything

—it was just a sprain, and his ankle was wrapped this morning. Do you think it could have been Joe? Could it have been his voice?"

I tried to recall how the intruder sounded but so much was still blurry. "I don't know. I wish I did. I mean, the voice sounded kind of familiar, but . . . I'm just not sure."

"We'll keep looking into it, Holly. Nothing else is going to happen."

"What are you going to do?" I desperately wanted to get out of here and go with him, but I knew that wouldn't be happening.

"I'm going to check to see if anyone found out anything about Brandon Garrison. We also have guys staking out Skippy's house. I feel like we're getting closer, Holly. I can sense it in my bones. There's no other reason someone would have done this to you unless we were— unless you—were getting close."

"I hope you're right." This was day three of Sarah being missing. Her medication would only last five more days. Time was quickly running out.

After I finished eating a midmorning snack—a banana and yogurt—someone knocked at my door.

I figured it was someone from my family, Drew, Chase, or Jamie.

Instead, a woman with long curly hair and shifty eyes stepped into my room, closed the door, and turned toward me.

I sucked in a quick breath.

It was the woman from the photo. The one who'd been with Sarah.

She was here. Alone with me. And moving my way with a distinct purpose in her steps.

I glanced at the nightstand for my phone, unsure if I should panic and call the police or wait.

"Please, I'm not going to hurt you." The woman raised a hand, reaching for me with a shake of her head.

I climbed up higher in bed, maybe in a subconscious way of making myself look bigger. Unfortunately, very few people looked intimidating in a hospital gown.

"What are you doing here?" My voice croaked out, cracking with each syllable.

She looked over her shoulder before stepping closer. "We need to talk."

I quickly studied her. She had curly hair—hair that could be fabulous with the right products. She wore a cheap flannel shirt, faded jeans, and dirty boots. No makeup.

I glanced at my phone again out of the corner of my eye. I could still grab it if I needed to. But would I have the chance to dial? Could I grab the call button and get a nurse here if I needed?

"Who are you?" I asked.

"I'm Lula . . . I'm Sarah's mom." Her eyes held a vast depth of sadness and pain as she stood beside me.

Realization rushed through me at her pronouncement. "Sarah has a picture with you."

"She took it when we met a few months ago."

"I didn't think she'd talked to you in years."

Lula glanced at her hands—hands with nubby nails and dirt wedged into the cracks. "I'm not supposed to have any contact with her. I lost all of my custodial rights. I was deeply involved in the drug culture, and I would have rathered buy heroin for myself than insulin for my daughter. I'm ashamed of the person I was."

"Okay . . ." I wasn't sure where she was going with this or why she was here or what she was planning.

"I've been clean for more than a year now. I went to rehab. I tried to turn my life around."

"The police can't find anything on you. They've been looking, hoping you had some answers."

"I changed my last name. Unofficially, of course. I thought if I did that, that maybe I'd have a real chance at starting over." Premature wrinkles brought about by a hard life—and most likely smoking—pulled across her face.

"I'm still not sure why you're here, Lula." My gut told me she wouldn't hurt me, but I still couldn't be certain. I was vulnerable right now, and I had to be careful.

She let out a deep sigh and pulled her sleeves over her hands, that pensive expression still on her face. "A year after I took my last hit and started the process of changing my life, I decided I wanted to connect with Sarah and tell her how sorry I was for the pain I'd caused her. I knew the social worker probably wouldn't go for it. So I took matters into my own hands."

"How did you do that?" Had those measures been drastic? Dangerous?

"I slipped a phone to Sarah. I paid a student at the school to give it to her."

"One of her friends?" My mind instantly ran through their faces. Had another one of them been hiding something from me?

"No, just a random student that I caught outside the school."

"What next?" I licked my dry lips, wondering where this was going.

"There was a note with the phone asking her to wait for a call at four that afternoon. She waited and was . . . surprisingly happy to hear from me. I didn't know how she would react or if she would be open to reconnecting with me."

"You eventually met up, I assume, since you have a picture together." I tried to put together a timeline in my head.

Lula nodded. "That's right. I asked if I could take

Sarah for coffee. Any time she wanted. She could name the place. I just wanted to see my baby. She said she would meet me at lunch one day. It was a school day, but she said she could leave the campus for forty-five minutes."

That would have been when Tina was her foster mom. I would bet Tina had no clue this had gone on.

"It was so wonderful to see her," Lula said, tears springing to her eyes. "She's grown into a fine young lady."

"I agree. Did you keep seeing her after that initial meeting?"

"No, but we talked on the phone in between her classes. She really liked you, Holly. You were good for her."

Well, at least there was that. It did mean something considering I felt like such a failure as a foster mom. But this conversation wasn't about me. "Did you tell Sarah to keep the phone private?"

Lula swung her head back and forth. "No, that was her idea. She wasn't sure people would approve. I paid the monthly bill, though, and she kept the phone hidden in the locker at school."

I was certain she hadn't come here to tell me all of this. "Why are you here now, Lula? What's going on?"

Her face twisted with grief. "Because I waited for Sarah to call me yesterday. She never did. I got worried

217

and started doing some research. That's when I heard she was missing. I've been beside myself."

I studied her face, looking for any sign of deceit. I didn't see any indicators. "You have any idea what happened, Lula? We've been looking for her, and I'm worried."

"No. The last time we talked, Sarah told me she might start doing some work for an internet company of some sort. I told her not to, that she didn't need to work yet and that there were better ways to get money."

"And she said?"

"I think she'd changed her mind and was going to tell the guy no. She said maybe other opportunities would come along." Lula's face crumpled into a sob. "I'm worried about her, Holly. I'm really worried about her. I think you're the only other person who understands me when I say that Sarah would never leave like this on her own. Never."

CHAPTER 27

"I KNOW Sarah wouldn't just leave like this. That's why I'm committed to finding her."

"Thank you, Holly." Lula wiped the moisture beneath her eyes using the sleeve of her shirt.

"Do you have any idea why she wanted to earn her own money?" My voice climbed higher, though I tried to stop it. But this just didn't make sense to me. "I don't understand. All of Sarah's needs were taken care of."

"She wanted to send the money to me, I think," Lula said. "I told her not to. But she thought if I could get back on my feet, maybe we would have the chance at being a family again."

I wasn't sure why a touch of betrayal sliced through my heart, but it did. Still, the end goal was always to bring families back together. Always—as long as the conditions were safe and healthy.

I suppose I'd envisioned Sarah staying with me . . . not moving on. I didn't want to send her to another foster family, so it had seemed like a given. I'd never envisioned Lula showing up.

And maybe this was my problem. My current thoughts always jumped ahead to thoughts of the future and what I wanted it to look like. But things rarely worked out the way I wanted.

Besides, if the doctors were right . . . if something was wrong with me . . . then maybe this would be for the best. A lump formed in my throat at the thought.

Don't go there right now, Holly. Don't go there.

I cleared my throat, trying to push away my emotions. "Why are you telling me this instead of the police, Lula?"

Lula's expression hardened. "Anyone who's been on the street for a while will tell you that they don't like cops. I'm no different. I've had too many bad run-ins. My criminal record is too long. Besides, I don't have anything to offer them."

"But you're here now. I'm still not certain why."

"Because I need for you to find my girl."

"I've been trying." My thoughts shifted. "What about Sarah's dad? Do you think he has anything to do with this?"

"Gary? I haven't seen him in years. He's locked up,

and he will be for a long time. He was a drug dealer. Claimed he did it so we could have the money to take care of our girl. But he got high one night and got into a fight. Killed the man."

My stomach clenched at the thought. "So you don't think he'd have anything to do with this?"

"No. Nothing."

Just then the door to my room opened, and Lula darted away before I could say anything else.

Drew pointed his thumb over his shoulder toward the door as Lula disappeared. "Who was that?"

"It's a long story," I said, still chewing on everything she'd told me.

He stood beside me and took my hand, appearing bright-eyed in his button-up shirt and slacks. No doubt he had a tie and matching suit coat in his car. "I'll hear about it another time then. Have you heard anything from the doctor yet?"

"No, not yet. Who knows how long the test results will take to get back." I was trying not to think about it, but I could see the mental storm clouds coming from the distance.

"It feels like forever, even though it's only been less than a day since this nightmare started."

"I know."

Drew offered a sad smile before pulling up a chair and sitting beside me. "How are you holding up, Holly?"

"I'm doing okay." If I stopped to think for long enough, I'd remember all my fears and anxieties, and I would no longer be okay. That was why I tried not to think about them, lest worry consume me whole.

Drew swallowed hard and lowered his voice, like he had something important to say. "Holly, I'm sorry about the altercation between Chase and me yesterday. It wasn't what you needed to awake to after your ordeal."

"No, it wasn't." There was no need to disagree. The whole confrontation had been upsetting on more than one level.

"I need to ask you something." Drew pulled in a deep breath, and I knew that whatever it was, it was heavy on his mind and difficult to say.

Part of me dreaded hearing it. But if it was important to Drew, it was important to me.

"Okay. Go ahead."

His gaze locked onto mine. "I need you to stay away from Chase."

I sucked in a breath. I hadn't expected to hear that. "What?"

Drew glanced at the window, as if gathering his thoughts before looking back at me. "I know it sounds selfish, Holly. But if you and I are going to work, Chase can't be in your life."

A rising sense of panic started in me. "He's hardly in my life. He's the detective on the case. There's a difference."

Drew gave me a skeptical glance and lowered his voice even more. "You know he's more than that."

"He's a friend."

"He's an ex-boyfriend, someone who broke your heart."

"But Chase and I are done." Why were my defenses rising? It was stupid, really. But they were up, and I couldn't get them back down. Not without a fight.

"Are you? Because every time I'm around the two of you, I sense there are unfinished things. I know the breakup was hard on you."

"Drew, I'm committed to you." I locked gazes with Drew, silently begging him to believe me.

He drew in a deep breath and licked his lips.

"Holly, regardless of your past or if you are committed to me, I still need you to cut Chase out of your life." His voice left no room for debate. No, he'd said the words with absolute certainty. But I was going to debate anyway.

"But—"

"I'm not forcing you, Holly. You're your own woman."

My heart ached at the thought. "But if I don't?"

"Then I don't see how we can truly be a couple."

My heart sagged. Ached. Felt ripped in two.

"What do you say?" Drew quietly asked.

Committed. You're committed, Holly. You're supposed to make sacrifices for the ones you love. What if you were in Drew's shoes and one of his ex-girlfriends started to hang around? You'd appreciate it if he did the same for you.

So why did I still feel unconvinced?

Emotion, I remembered. I was letting my emotion get in my way.

"I'll need to talk to Chase again," I finally said. "I have some things I need to tell him before I put that space there."

"I understand." Drew smiled, his whole demeanor looking more relaxed now. "Thank you, Holly. I appreciate that you care about me enough to respect my opinion."

"Of course."

But deep inside, I didn't like this. Not one bit.

And that could end up being a problem.

CHAPTER 28

DREW TOOK me home a few hours later and got me settled on my couch with a blanket, some tea, and cookies.

His concern for me was sweet. But I was trying to hold back my resentment. The clash between emotional and rational had given me a pulsating headache.

I supposed I hadn't realized it until now, but I wasn't a fan of ultimatums.

I also knew Drew had a point. Being with Chase *had* stirred up old memories. And though I fought them and tried to keep myself in check, maybe I was entering dangerous territory.

"Are you comfortable?" Drew asked, kneeling beside me.

I nodded and raised my teacup. "I am. You should go to work. I need to rest anyway."

"I don't mind staying." His brown eyes were warm with concern and sincerity.

"I know you don't. But I'll be okay."

He kissed my forehead and disappeared out the door. As soon as he was gone, I called Jamie. There would be time for rest later. She promised to come right over and showed up ten minutes later with a bag of chocolate-covered almonds and my favorite coffee. Those who knew me best could speak my love language so well.

"Thank you," I told her.

She sat on the coffee table beside me, probably so she could get a better look at my face. "I've been dying to talk to you. I went to the hospital but they said you weren't taking any visitors. What's going on?"

I poured everything out to her, including the information about Sarah's mom and Drew's ultimatum. She was far more interested in Drew's ultimatum.

"He really said he didn't want you talking with Chase?"

I nodded, feeling sick to my stomach. "He did."

"I don't know if I admire him for having standards or if I dislike him for asking you to do that."

I clenched the blanket around me. "I suppose it makes sense, Jamie. Because there will always be a part of me that cares about Chase. I'm just trying not to focus on my emotions."

Jamie squinted and tilted her head to the side. "Girl, I know where you're coming from. I do. But don't you think that God gives us emotions for a reason? They're not useless, like eyebrows."

"Eyebrows aren't useless—never mind." I started to explain but stopped myself.

My friend's eyes lit. She'd made her point. "Exactly. Even eyebrows have a purpose. God is not a frivolous God. He even made mosquitoes for a reason."

I saw where she was going with this, but . . . "I just don't think we can let the whims of our hearts dictate our lives. Emotions lie to us. The heart lies to us, Jamie."

"I agree," Jamie said, slowly forming her words. "But emotions are often an indicator of what's going on inside us. That's all I want you to think about."

I sighed and popped an almond into my mouth. She had a point. Sometimes, things in life weren't so black-and-white. Usually our thoughts triggered the emotions, and our thoughts were generally grounded in our past experiences.

It wasn't as simple as my statements made it seem. Our feelings didn't determine truth. No, truth was unyielding and definite.

Yet my emotions were what blinded me right now.

The conundrum wasn't lost on me, and I sighed again.

"Maybe it is better if I don't talk to Chase anymore. I just need to call him, give him a final update, and then let him carry on without me."

She gave me one of her looks. "You really think you're going to be able to do that?"

I shrugged. "I have no idea."

It was the honest truth.

She set her coffee down. "I can answer that for you. No. Until Sarah's found, you're not going to drop this."

"Then let's talk about Sarah instead. We are running out of ideas, Jamie. I just have no idea where else to look. I've followed every lead and every crazy whim even. They've practically led me nowhere, except for a trip to the hospital. Sarah's dad—he's out. Cameron—he's out. Joe Richardson—also out. Brandon—he could be out, but I'm waiting to hear for sure."

"Maybe you should lie low," Jamie said. "For more than one reason. Your body is breaking down. This is affecting your relationship with Drew. You haven't been to work in a week. There are a lot of signs there that you should let this go."

"I'm not denying that."

"So what are you going to do?"

I knew I should say, "Let this go."

But I couldn't. Instead, I stared at Jamie and shrugged. "I'm going to keep searching, of course."

Before Jamie left, someone knocked on my door. Jamie answered for me, and I was surprised to see Cameron standing on the other side. I motioned for him to step inside, and Jamie closed the door, delaying her departure. Instead, she eyed my visitor with obvious distrust.

He looked terrible today. The circles under his eyes were darker and deeper. His acne somehow seemed brighter—or maybe his skin was paler. His hair seemed oily, and he was wearing the same outfit he'd had on when Chase questioned him two days ago.

"Cameron, what a surprise," I said. "How in the world did you know where I live or even what my name was?"

Cameron shrugged like the question was a no-brainer. "Sarah told me your name. And your address I got from Google, of course."

I really needed to make sure I took my address off the internet—if that was even possible. But that was beside the point right now.

I pushed myself up on the couch, thankful I'd taken the time to change and make myself a little more presentable after my hospital stay.

Jamie still remained standing at the door, almost like a guard who was ready to spring, if necessary.

"Is everything okay, Cameron?" My gaze darted back to him.

Cameron shook his head and sat down in the chair across from me. "I didn't know who else I could talk to."

How strange was it that I'd dug and dug, and I hadn't found any answers. And now that I wasn't digging, the answers were coming to me without any effort on my part—other than almost dying and possibly having a misdiagnosis misdiagnosed.

I was going to comfort myself with the thought that I had at least laid the groundwork for these answers.

Right?

"What's going on?" I asked, anxious to hear what he had to say.

"There's something I didn't tell you." He grabbed one of the cookies Jamie had put on my coffee table. "Do you mind?"

"Help yourself."

He took a bite. "These are really good."

"Thank you," I said uncertainly. "Would you like some milk too?"

"Oh, no. I'm good. Thanks."

The boy was certainly making himself at home.

When he didn't keep talking, I asked, "What do you need to tell me, Cameron?"

He lowered the cookie and frowned again. "Sarah called me the day she disappeared."

I narrowed my eyes. Why did people keep things like this quiet? Had they lost their minds? Irritation burned at me, but this wasn't the time for a lecture. No, I just needed to know about this conversation with Sarah.

"What did Sarah say?" I asked.

"She sounded panicked and said they didn't know she had a phone."

Alarm spiked in me. "Who is *they*?"

He shook his head a little too quickly. "Sarah . . . she didn't say. She told me not to tell anyone what was going on. She made me promise."

"Why? Why were you not supposed to tell anyone?" I could feel my blood pressure rising.

Cameron lowered the cookie back to the table, crumbs falling everywhere. "She said she thought she had an opportunity. It had sounded too good to be true, but if it worked out, she'd have found the solution she was praying for."

"Sounds pretty vague." Jamie took a step closer, her arms crossed and a skeptical slant to her voice.

"It was all a secret but . . . she feared she was going to be sent to another foster home if she messed up. That's why she didn't call you. She knew you'd be disappointed with her, and she couldn't handle being rejected again."

Grief pounded at my temples. I wouldn't reject her for making a mistake. I wish I could tell her that myself. That I could reassure her.

But that wasn't a possibility right now.

"I tried to get more details from her, but she said she

didn't have a lot of time," Cameron continued. "She started to tell me one other thing, but before she could finish the line went dead."

"What did she say before the line went dead, Cameron?" I held my breath as I waited for his answer.

He swallowed hard, his Adam's apple bobbing up and down. "She said they were going to use her like a lab rat, and she warned that I might be next."

CHAPTER 29

"WHAT DO YOU THINK THAT MEANS?" Jamie took Cameron's seat after he left, looking as confused as I felt. I took another sip of coffee, hoping it would magically make my brain work more efficiently. It didn't. "I have no idea. A lab rat? Jamie, this has to go back to her diabetes. It's the only thing that make sense."

Jamie wiped Cameron's cookie crumbs into a napkin and balled it into her hands. "You said one of the other foster kids who went missing had diabetes?"

"That's right. As well as one two years ago."

Jamie leaned back, obviously staying for a while. "The only person they have in common is that support group leader, right?"

"As far as I know. And maybe Family Services."

"Did these kids have the same social worker?"

"Kathy?" The very notion of my friend being involved felt like a slap in the face. "She wouldn't do this."

"You have to be objective. It can't hurt to verify that."

I nodded—even though I didn't want to. "You're right. I'll put in a call to one of my old colleagues and see what I can find out."

"We should check this Brandon guy out also."

"I agree." I started to stand, but Jamie pushed me backed own.

"You're supposed to rest." She raised an eyebrow and stared, daring me to argue.

"There's no way I can rest now. I can rest when Sarah is back. When I know she's okay."

"You're not going to be worth anything if you're dead."

Her words rang in my ears. "I'm not going to die."

Jamie's face fell into a frown and her sassiness disappeared. Her words had gotten to her, I realized. "I'm sorry, Holly. I didn't mean that. I just mean that you should take care of yourself. You look tired, and I think you've lost more weight. You're going to shrivel up to nothing."

"I'll be okay. Whatever happens, I'll be okay. God will save me from this fire. But even if He doesn't, I'll still trust Him."

"Oh, girlfriend, what would I do without you?" Tears sprang to Jamie's eyes, and she reached forward to give me a hug.

I clung to my best friend, on the verge of a breakdown. I hated to see my loved ones hurting because of me. Yet I was so thankful they were here to help carry my burdens.

I waited until Jamie pulled back, wiped her eyes, and pulled herself together.

She sucked in a shaky breath as she turned back to me. "Whew. I can't even deal right now."

My heart panged with grief. "I get that."

"Listen, I know once you get your mind set on something, I can't change it. But at least I said my piece, and you know how I feel."

"You did."

She crossed her arms. "So what now?"

"Let me call a friend at Family Services. Then I want to do some research on this Brandon guy."

"And Chase? Are you going to tell him?"

Dread pooled in my gut. "I will. It makes sense to keep him in the loop."

"Are you going to tell him that you can't talk to him anymore after that?"

"*After that* being the key words. I need to complete this case first, Jamie. Drew will understand."

"Are you going to tell Drew that?"

"Yes," I said. "It's only fair."

"Okay, it's your call. And it's your lucky day because I have the rest of the day off work, and Wesley is out of town, so I'm at your disposal."

"Just like old times?"

Jamie smiled "Just like old times."

Jamie ran to pick up lunch. I had just enough time to call a friend at Family Services, but she wasn't in, so I left a message. As soon as I put my phone down, Chase arrived. I hadn't known he was coming, but it would be good for us to talk. At least we'd have a little privacy.

My heart sank when I remembered Drew's words. I wanted to respect him and honor our relationship. To honor my word.

But was he asking more than I could handle? And, if that was the case, was I even ready to get married? Marriage . . . well, it was a whole different ballgame than dating. I thought I was fairly mature . . . but maybe I wasn't. Otherwise, I wouldn't feel so conflicted.

"How are you, Holly?" Chase sat in the chair across from me, consuming the small piece of furniture.

The sight almost made me smile—until I remembered the reason he was here.

"I'm okay," I said, ignoring the exhaustion that tugged at my eyelids. "Just glad to be home from the hospital."

"You need to take care of yourself," he warned.

"People keep saying that, but I feel like I am taking care of myself."

He gave me a pointed glance. "Maybe you need someone to take care of you."

My throat went dry at his words. What was he implying? I wasn't sure, and I couldn't bring myself to ask if he was volunteering for the task.

"There are a few things I need to talk to you about," I told him, pulling a pillow into my lap. Was this my subconscious way of creating a barrier? Maybe.

"Of course. Anything. But first I want to let you know that I talked to Brandon Garrison. He said he was at the hospital so late last night because he'd left his inhaler in his desk. He's an asthmatic, apparently. The video footage did show that he stayed only ten minutes."

"That would have been long enough to hit me with the stun gun."

"True . . . but it's going to be difficult to prove that. We're still looking."

"Okay, my turn now." I started by telling him about Lula's unexpected appearance and then moved on to Cameron's visit and my newest theories.

He let out a long breath, as if impressed. "You've been praying for answers, haven't you?"

"I have, actually."

"It looks like those answers are starting to pour in. Thanks for letting me know." He paused, and I could tell he was thinking. "I don't understand why Sarah would call herself a lab rat."

"I'm not sure either. But I think that confirms this has something to do with her disease. All of it does."

"Not necessarily. She could be a product tester. It could be another scheme to make money by doing a study for medical students at the college—something as simple as how many hot dogs a person can eat in an hour or how long a person can go without sleep."

"Maybe, but it seems unlikely."

He leaned back. "Let's say it is centered on diabetes, for some reason. Why would a crime be centered on that disease, unless it's making money by selling the supplies needed? Skippy has been cleared. He's not behind this. He was filming a YouTube video of himself playing Fortnight. It's time-stamped."

"I have no idea. I'm hoping you can figure it out."

"I'll do my best." He studied me a minute, his eyes seeming to stare into my soul. "Is there something else?"

"Drew doesn't want me talking to you anymore," I blurted. I hadn't intended on saying it that way. There were much more elegant, graceful ways of wording it. But the truth had just poured out before I could stop—unhindered and clumsy.

Chase's eyebrows rose, and he nodded slowly. "I see. What do you think about that?"

"Your friendship means a great deal to me, Chase." My throat burned as the words left my lips.

"But you can't have both." He said the words evenly, softly.

I glanced at my lap to where my fingers were folded together, almost as if in prayer. "Apparently not."

"I can understand where he's coming from, Holly. And I respect his wishes."

My pulse jumped. I hadn't expected him to say that. "What about my wishes?"

He paused, his gaze still latched to mine. "What do you mean?"

What *did* I mean? And how much of what I meant did I say? "I mean, I don't know what I want to do."

"Are you breaking up with Drew?"

"No." I cared about Drew. I really did.

"Then we can't be friends, Holly. Not if you want to maintain your relationship with Drew." Chase frowned, and his face looked stoic and hard.

"But—"

"I'm not going to be the one who messes things up for you. I won't let myself be that person. You deserve better."

"But—"

"From now on, maybe you should contact Colerain if you have any new leads or if you have questions."

I didn't *want* to talk to Colerain. I wanted to talk to Chase. But if I argued this too much, I was just going to sound like a whiny baby—and that was never becoming of a woman.

"I'm going to tell Drew that I need to be in contact with you until this investigation is over," I finally said, raising my chin with stubborn determination. "Then I'll make some changes."

"How do you think Drew is going to handle that?"

"Hopefully, like a man."

He stood, an instant—but unseen—barrier appearing between the two of us. "You need your rest, Holly. If you interfere in this investigation again, I'll have to take definitive measures."

Panic started inside me. "What do you mean?"

"I mean, I can't put you at risk. Drew was right. It's too dangerous. You're out of this, Holly."

He couldn't be serious. "But—"

He leveled his gaze. "I mean it, Holly."

"What do you mean by definitive measures?"

"It means I'll do whatever I have to do to ensure you stay away, even if I have to press charges for impeding a police investigation."

Resentment rose in me. I wasn't sure if it was directed

at Chase or Drew. Or maybe at both. But I didn't like how all of this was playing out.

As Chase walked away, I felt like he was taking a piece of my soul with him.

Which probably meant him leaving was the best idea. But I still hated it.

CHAPTER 30

"WHAT DID you find out about Brandon?" I asked Jamie thirty minutes later.

We'd set out to divide and conquer—all while in the safety of my home and utilizing the strengths of the internet. Some coffee, lunch, and good music had helped to make everything better—temporarily, at least. I couldn't get arrested for doing this.

I didn't think.

Jamie had her computer in her lap as we sat at my kitchen table. She'd downed a salad while I'd attempted to eat a grilled chicken sandwich and fruit.

"I don't know, Holly." She let out a long breath and stared at her computer. "From everything I've been able to find, he seems like an upright kind of guy."

"So do most serial killers. Keep digging."

"Whoa." She raised an eyebrow. "Listen to you, talking about serial killers like that."

I released my breath. I knew I sounded impatient. "I'm sorry. There's just got to be a lead here somewhere."

She tapped in a few more things on the computer before shaking her head. "Holly, I don't think he's our guy."

"Why would you say that?"

"For starters, he has kids at home. He volunteers. Goes to church."

"Doesn't mean he's not guilty."

"But if someone is using Sarah as a lab rat, then how would Brandon be involved? He doesn't have enough education to formulate anything that would help these kids."

"He was a nurse."

"Okay, well, that fact aside—according to his social media, he was out of town when Sarah went missing. He was presenting a workshop at a conference down in Alabama. I doubt he could get back in time to be involved with this."

She had a valid point.

"Then who?" I asked.

She sighed and leaned back. "I don't know. Are we convinced this has something to do with the diabetes?"

"I'm inclined to think so. The more I learn, the more I

think someone with some background in the disease has to be involved."

"So someone who has a background in diabetes and who might want to use kids who've been cast away by society for lab rats." She frowned. "I sound like I'm in the middle of some bad conspiracy theory."

"But maybe not. This might be real." The answer lingered at the back of my mind. There was someone I was missing. I was certain of it.

"Cameron is out. Joe Richardson is out. The guy buying and selling diabetic test strips is out. And now Brandon is out also." Jamie ticked people off on her fingers. "That doesn't leave us with anyone else—unless I'm missing something."

I leaned back and tried my hardest to think of who else might be involved here. And when it hit me, I nearly doubled over. "Jamie . . ."

"What is it?"

"I know who it could be." The ideas swirled in my head, but I didn't have time to make sense of them. I just needed to talk it out. "Dr. Marks."

Jamie made a face, showing her clear confusion. "Who's Dr. Marks?"

"He's the endocrinologist that Sarah was seeing. He's one of the most well-known in the country."

Her confusion turned to skepticism. "Okay. Doctors are usually in the business of helping people."

"I know. Exactly. What better way to help them than by finding a cure?"

"It's extreme."

"We don't have any better ideas right now. So just hear me out." I sat up straighter as my theory came to life in my mind.

"I'm listening."

"We need to find out if those missing foster kids saw him as a physician. If he's the connection."

She nodded slowly. "That's a valid idea."

"We need to find out everything we can about him, for that matter. He's been right in front of me this whole time, I just haven't seen him as a suspect." I looked at my friend. "Listen, can you find out if he might be the doctor for these kids?"

"How am I supposed to do that?"

Great question. I thought for a minute when the perfect idea hit me.

"Call the doctor's office and ask if you can make an appointment for Avril White. They'll ask if she's a new patient. Say no, that she was last seen five months ago. They should look her up in their system and confirm that —or not."

"Great idea."

I thought it was a pretty nifty idea myself. "In the meantime, I'm going to call my brother–in-law. Maybe he knows something about Dr. Marks that will help."

"It can't hurt to try," Jamie said, picking up her phone. "I'll see what I can find out."

I abandoned my post on the couch and went back to my bedroom so our conversations wouldn't cross.

William—Alex's husband—was a general surgeon. He was pretty quiet and tight-lipped most of the time, but occasionally I could get information from him. I hoped now was one of those times.

"Everyone knows Dr. Marks," William told me.

"They do?" I'd never heard this before. Then again, I'd never brought the doctor up. I'd never had reason to.

"He's very well respected in his field."

"What else do you know about him?" I sat on my bed and ran my hand across the white coverlet, trying to get the wrinkles out.

He paused. "Why are you asking this, Holly?"

"I'm just curious." It was a lame excuse, but it had been the first thing that came to mind.

"Your curiosity usually turns into something bigger than that." He sighed. "Either way, yes, Dr. Marks seems like an upright kind of guy. He's smart and at the top of his game."

"Do you know if he's always been a practicing doctor? Or has he done research at some point?"

"I'm not sure, Holly. I do remember some kind of article about him that came out a couple of years ago. He was on the edge of some breakthrough research, but I don't know what came of it." He paused. "Now, do you want to tell me what's going on? This is more than mere curiosity."

"Would you be offended if I said no?"

"I wouldn't be surprised. Offended? We're beyond that stage of our relationship. And you're supposed to be resting."

"I am resting. Talking to you is very relaxing." I frowned at my words. They didn't sound very convincing, not even to me.

"Holly . . ."

"Just trust me. I'm fine. And thank you for your concern."

He paused. "I heard what happened. Did you get the tests back yet?"

I stared at the sunny day out my window, wishing my spirit felt that bright and cheerful. "You know how long these things take."

"Yes, I do. Let me know when you hear, okay? Alex is worried about you."

"I will. Thanks, William."

As soon as I hung up, I went to my computer at the kitchen table and typed the doctor's name into Google search. Yes, Google. The all-knowing search engine that was both a blessing and a curse.

Pages of results came up. I searched through several until I found what I was looking for.

Dr. Marks had worked for a company called the Bayside Project and had, indeed, been on the edge of groundbreaking research. However, for undisclosed reasons, the funding was pulled for his project, and he was fired. Afterward, he went back to being a practicing physician.

That didn't necessarily point to wrongdoing on his part. There were multiple reasons that funding could be pulled, I supposed.

But something still bothered me about all of this.

Jamie put her phone down and smiled. "Guess what? Your idea worked. Avril is one of Dr. Marks's patients. You are on fire, hotter than a flea in a frying pan."

Was that a good thing? And how did this all add up?

I wasn't sure yet.

But all I knew was that this was worth investigating, and that meant that step two would involve leaving the house and forgoing rest for a bit longer.

CHAPTER 31

"SO, we're just going to find Dr. Marks's house and sit outside of it?" Jamie asked, giving me one of her diva-like glances as we headed to the Cincinnati suburbs thirty minutes later. "Watch the house? Pray over the house? What exactly are you thinking?"

I shrugged. "There are many options. I'm not sure which one is best yet."

She pulled into his neighborhood. "This area isn't that fancy for a doctor—especially for someone who's a specialist and world-renowned like he is."

It wasn't. The homes were older, smaller, and not well-maintained.

"I agree," I said. "Maybe he gives his money to charity and lives on less."

"While also being a child abductor?" Jamie gave me a look.

I shrugged. "I don't know. But what I do know is that he had access to the hospital where I was attacked. That he has a connection with at least two of the three missing foster kids in this area. And that funding was pulled for his research project. It sounds like a home run to me."

"But why would he abduct these kids? What's his motive? It's so drastic."

"Maybe he's desperate. Maybe he feels like he can give them the care they need. Maybe . . . maybe he's psychotic and this is filling some kind of need that will never make sense to anyone." I really hated that explanation and hoped it wasn't true. "Maybe there's an entirely different reason. Really, there's so much I don't know."

"Sarah told Cameron something about being a lab rat."

"I . . . I know." I shuddered. "I just don't want to think about what that means."

Jamie turned her attention back to the street, but her frown remained. "And why'd you bring me instead of someone else?"

"You mean instead of Chase?" I pointed to the upcoming street where she needed to turn.

"I mean, instead of Drew."

I nearly snorted. "This isn't the kind of case for Drew. He just tries to fix things."

"Most men do."

"I don't want him to try to fix me. I want him to support me. To brainstorm with me. To let me explore crazy leads that might not pan out."

"And I guess he doesn't do that?"

"No, he doesn't do that. He's too straight-laced for it."

"And to think I always saw you with a straight-laced kind of guy."

"I am with a straight-laced kind of guy. I'm with Drew. Have you forgotten that?"

"Nope, I didn't forget."

She didn't say anything.

I didn't ask.

We stopped in front of a 1950s-style home. The doctor wasn't here right now. No, he was at the office where he supposedly worked until six. We'd double-checked with the office staff.

That gave me three hours.

"So, what's your decision? Stare at an empty house?" Jamie asked. "Or did you have something else in mind?"

"No, I'm planning on doing something far worse." My palms felt sweaty just thinking about it.

Jamie's eyes widened. "What's that?"

I swallowed hard, bracing myself for Jamie's response. "I'm breaking in."

Jamie swung her head back and forth. "Oh no, girl.

That's a bad idea. A bad, bad idea. Don't you remember what happened in the past when we did that?"

It was hard for me to forget the time I'd found that dead body. I didn't want a repeat, but . . . "It's the only way."

"You could get arrested. Didn't we agree you don't want to get arrested? Or die?"

I stared at the house, picturing what I was about to do. It was risky—but big things required risk. "If I'm not caught I won't be arrested or die."

Jamie crossed her arms in defiance. "You don't think this doctor has a security system?"

I stared harder at the house, observing all the details. "There aren't any signs on his windows. Besides, if the security system goes off, I'll run and you'll take off."

She nodded slowly, thoughtfully—but still didn't look convinced. "So I'm not going in with you?"

I turned toward my friend and frowned. "No, I wouldn't ask you to do that."

"I appreciate that, but I'll still be an accessory to your crime." She released a long breath. "What if someone sees you? Did you think of that?"

I pulled my gaze back toward the house. The older neighborhood had larger yards with more foliage than the newer neighborhoods. "There are trees on either side of the house. It's pretty private. Besides, I wore a cleaning uniform—"

"That's a cleaning uniform?" Jamie gave me a skeptical glance as she looked me up and down.

I brushed off the blue button-up shirt I wore with a black skirt and canvas tennis shoes. "It's a cute cleaning uniform, but yes. Anyway, *and* you're driving your van."

We usually called the beat-up minivan the Ghettomobile. Need I explain more?

"I would be insulted, but I can't be."

I'd known she wouldn't be insulted or I wouldn't have said it. "I think I can come up with a decent cover story, if push comes to shove."

"That's why you brought a bucket." Realization stretched through her voice.

"Of course. Why would you ask?"

"I thought you might be doing a random act of kindness again."

"No. I mean, I do still love those. But not if they require something illegal. For the most part."

"The girl's so idealistic that she'll break the law if it means accomplishing what she's set out to do," Jamie muttered. "I don't know if that's admirable or stupid."

"Probably a bit of both." I squeezed the handle. "Okay, you stay here. Let me know if you hear anything, Girl Genius."

"You too, Retro Girl." Those were the names we'd used for each other when I'd gotten myself in trouble the first time by breaking into someone's house to clean it for them. The problem was that I'd found a dead body in the process.

That wouldn't be the case this time.

I hoped.

With a mop and bucket in my hand, I rattled the front door.

It was locked, just as I thought it would be.

But I'd come with a plan.

I pulled out my lock-picking kit. My dad had been a locksmith, and he'd taught me some of the tricks of the trade.

Just as I heard the click I'd been waiting for, my phone rang. I glanced at the screen.

Chase.

I didn't have time to talk to him now.

Instead, I slipped inside the house.

My heart was pounding out of control. I could get in serious trouble. Tarnish my family's good name. Cause Drew to rethink our relationship.

So many things could go wrong here.

But it was worth the risk if I found Sarah.

I glanced around. I didn't see anything indicating there was an alarm here. I took that as a good sign.

I paused for just a moment to look at a picture on his

mantel. It was of Dr. Marks with a young girl who looked about twelve. His arm was around her, and they both smiled wildly.

I squinted as I picked it up and examined the picture more closely.

Was that an insulin pump on the girl?

I couldn't be sure. I put the photo back down, noting that there were no photos of the doctor with any women. I assumed that meant he was single, and I stored those facts away to the back of my mind.

I didn't have much time, so I slipped toward the back of the house. I figured an office or a basement would be the best place to start.

The problem was, I didn't even know what I was looking for.

I passed his living room. He apparently liked to golf, based on a few knickknacks around the place. He liked fruit because there was a heaping wooden bowl of bananas and grapes and apples and oranges. It seemed like way too much for one man to eat, but who was I to judge?

A few rooms later, I came upon his office. I slipped inside and tapped the keyboard to his computer. It was locked. Of course.

I opened the drawers to his desk. There was nothing but his own personal paperwork—mostly house stuff and insurance, it appeared. Nothing that gave me any sign as to what was going on or if he was guilty.

This man was smart—obviously so. If he had anything that might incriminate him, would he keep it here?

Probably not.

Out of curiosity, I began to ruffle through some of his receipts. His financial information.

Nothing, nothing, nothing.

But I paused when I got to his electric bill.

The weird thing was, this house wasn't the address that was listed here on the bill.

No, it was in another county.

I took my phone out and took a picture.

As soon as I did, my phone buzzed.

It was Jamie.

SOS. He's back. Get out!

CHAPTER 32

MOVING QUICKLY, I slipped out the back door and circled around the side of the house. I spotted Dr. Marks by the front door, looking through his keys.

I held my breath as I waited and watched.

Finally, he jammed his key into the door and stepped inside. As soon as he did, I darted toward the tree line at the edge of the property. Swiftly, I jogged toward Jamie's van and jumped inside.

She took off before I even closed the door or put my seatbelt on.

I pressed myself into the seat and tried to catch my breath. My heart still pounded out of control and my hands shook. That had been close. Too close.

"Girl . . ." Jamie warned, glancing over at me as she headed out of the neighborhood.

"I know." She didn't have to spell out just how close that had been.

I rubbed my temples. My head swam again, and the world around me wobbled.

No, not another spell. Not now.

I squeezed my eyes shut, trying to fight it. It was no use.

Please, don't black out. No more blackouts.

"Holly, are you okay?" Worry tinged my friend's voice.

"I'm fine," I muttered, completely uncertain if I was really fine or not. "Keep going. Please."

"Should I take you to the hospital?"

I rubbed my temples again and took several deep gulps of air. "No, I just need a minute for this to pass."

We continued down the road. The seconds ticked by. My prayers continued.

After several moments, my world righted, and I opened my eyes again. I blinked. Sucked in air before exhaling it.

"Holly?" Jamie asked, concern still lining her words.

I blinked again, making sure the spell really had ended. It had. "I really am fine. I just had a minute."

Jamie didn't look convinced. "I'm sure I won't be able to talk you into going to the hospital, will I?"

"Nope. Sorry." I wasn't sure what my future held, but I wasn't ready for it to involve long hospital stays. My to-do list was calling, and finding Sarah was at the very top.

She glanced at me again, and I could tell she was still worried. "Did you find out anything, at least?"

I pulled out my phone and found the photo I'd taken. "I . . . I found an address. It's for a place about an hour from here. The doctor is paying the electricity there. I don't know if it means anything or not."

"But you want to find out?"

"Of course." I plugged in the address on my phone and told her where to turn. Then I studied the bill. "It's weird. Dr. Marks's name isn't on this bill, and it was sent to a post office box. Yet the bill itself was clearly in his possession."

"Should we tell Chase?" Jamie asked.

I remembered our last conversation. "I can't. He said he would arrest me if I interfered—and breaking into the doctor's house was definitely interfering."

"I get that, but I'm not interested in dying today. We may need backup."

"I'm not interested in dying today, either." But I might not have much choice. Waiting for the doctor's update on my health was killing me. It could be a life-changing conversation, and I wasn't sure I was prepared to face it.

I loved Jesus. I'd accepted Him as my Savior. I believed in salvation. In heaven.

But I just didn't feel ready to go yet.

Maybe it was better if I kept myself busy. Otherwise, my thoughts went places they shouldn't—places that weren't filled with peace, but instead were crowded with anxiety and burdensome emotions that wanted to overtake me.

I pointed to a road where Jamie needed to turn. As I did, a realization hit me.

"Jamie," I whispered.

"What is it?"

"I left my mop and bucket in the doctor's house."

I couldn't get the realization out of my head. How could I have been so stupid? What was Dr. Marks going to think? Were my prints on the bucket and mop? Would he call the police? Have them dust the supplies for DNA evidence?

"Stop beating yourself up," Jamie said.

"How can I not beat myself up? He knows someone was in his house now. I totally showed my hand."

"He doesn't know it was you."

"But he could find out. And the fact that he knows someone was in his house will make him suspicious. Maybe even reactive." I hung my head. "I don't know what I was thinking."

"You were thinking you had to get out of there. Better that he found that bucket than he found you."

"I can't argue with that." My phone rang, and I stared at the screen.

"Well, who is it?" Jamie asked.

"Chase."

"Aren't you going to answer?"

"I'm not sure what to say. He made it clear I shouldn't get involved."

"If you don't answer he'll be suspicious."

I sighed. She was right. But I was going to have to choose my words very carefully. "Hey, Chase."

"I hope I didn't wake you," he said.

"No, no. You didn't."

"What are you doing?" Was that suspicion in his voice? I glanced at Jamie. "I'm just hanging out with Jamie."

"Good. I'm proud of you, Holly. I figured you wouldn't give up and would keep trying to find answers, despite everything."

I let out a nervous laugh. "Me? Don't be silly."

Jamie cut me a look.

"I know I sounded harsh earlier, and I'm sorry. I just don't want to see you get hurt. And I don't want to be the one who messes up your future."

"I appreciate that. Is that the reason you called?" This wasn't the time or place to get into a deeper discussion about our earlier conversation. Besides, I had too many other things on my mind.

"Listen, I know I told you not to get involved, but I thought I'd give you an update. Maybe if you realize the police really are working on this case, you won't feel like you have to."

"Maybe. What did you find out?"

"I've been reviewing the list that Brandon Garrison sent me, the one of guest speakers for the support group. It turns out that doctor we ran into at the hospital—"

"Dr. Marks?" My pulse spiked.

"Yes, he's the one. He's apparently spoken at the support group on multiple occasions."

"Has he?" I glanced over at Jamie. "Are you going to check him out?"

"I am. I just thought you'd want to know."

"Thanks, Chase." I ended the call and put the phone in my lap.

"Well?" Jamie asked.

I relayed the conversation.

"You didn't tell him what we found?" she asked.

"If I told him, I'd have to also admit that I broke in. How am I going to explain that? Hopefully, he'll discover all this for himself soon."

We spotted the street from the electric bill, and Jamie stopped just before reaching the house.

This was it. The moment of truth. Would I find answers here? Or was all of this for nothing?

CHAPTER 33

I PULLED out some binoculars and studied the house in front of me. The ranch-style home was on a large plot of land with woods surrounding it on three sides. The nearest neighbor was a considerable distance away, making this place isolated.

The building itself wasn't fancy. There were no flower beds, just a wide stretch of grass in the front lawn. The shutters and siding on the house were painted a yellowish-beige, and the bricks were a peach color.

Nothing about it screamed dangerous or unsafe.

"Binoculars? What else do you have in that bag of tricks?" Jamie asked.

"My lock-picking kit. A wig. A fake gun. Why?"

Jamie snorted. "Girl, you are something else. You know that?"

"So I've been told." I kept looking, watching for a sign of movement at the house.

"You know, maybe we're thinking too hard here." Jamie tapped her finger against the steering wheel as she stared at the house also. "Maybe this place is a rental—some supplemental income—and it has nothing to do with this case."

"Why does Dr. Marks have a different name on the bill then?"

"That I cannot tell you. Maybe this place belongs to a relative, and Dr. Marks is helping out by paying his bills. There could be numerous explanations. Just because he's treated two patients and pays a mysterious electric bill doesn't mean he's also a child abductor."

"I agree. But while we're here, we should just check things out, right?"

She frowned. "I suppose."

As we sat in Jamie's van, waiting for our next step, I typed in the doctor's name on my phone one more time. This time, I wanted to know more about his personal life instead of his professional achievements.

It took weeding through several pages before I found what I was looking for. And it was a doozy.

"Jamie, Dr. Marks's daughter died from ketoacidosis." My stomach churned as I said the words.

"What?"

I nodded as compassion collided with realization

inside me. "Five years ago. She was only thirteen when it happened. Dr. Marks was apparently out of town, and the daughter had gone to a friend's house when she went into a diabetic coma and ultimately died."

"That's horrible."

"It really is. But it gives him motive, Jamie." I knew I shouldn't sound so excited, but I'd finally found the link I'd been searching for.

"Or it gives him a sad story." Jamie gave me one of her pointed looks.

"Maybe. I'm going to go check things out." I opened my door, tired of talking and speculating. This was the time to do something.

"Wait, I'm going with you." Jamie scrambled to grab my arm. "I can't let you go up there alone. And you should call Colerain first."

"You think I should?"

"Yes, I think you should. Like I said, I don't want to die today."

I nibbled on my bottom lip. I wanted to call Chase, but I couldn't bring myself to do it. Finally, I nodded. "Okay, I'll call him and tell him I got a lead and that he should check out this house."

"Thank you."

I dialed his number, but it went to voice mail. I frowned but finally decided I would leave a message for him. After I ended the call, I turned to my friend. "Deed done. Now I'm going to check the house out."

Jamie grabbed my arm again. "Maybe you should wait."

"What if Sarah is inside? She needs help, and I don't want to waste another minute. You don't have to come, Jamie. I'd never forgive myself if something happened to you."

"I'm not sending you to do this by yourself." She put her van in Drive, a determined look on her face. "I just need to find somewhere to park."

She pulled off into what appeared to be an old access road leading through the woods, probably set up for hunters, if I had to guess. At least the van would be out of sight, just in case anyone came past. We didn't want to raise suspicions.

"You're sure you're okay with this?" I asked her quietly as she took her keys from the ignition.

"Of course. I'm Jamie Duke, and I'm ready to conquer the world. Besides, what's a wannabee investigator without her trusted sidekick?"

I smiled. "Thanks, Jamie. But you've never been a sidekick—more like a partner."

We climbed out and cut through the woods toward the house. The area was hilly and thick with trees but manageable. Finally, we reached a clearing, and I spotted the house in the distance.

"There are no cars outside it—none that I can see." I peered around the low-lying branches of an oak tree.

"But there is a garage. One could be inside."

"True. We can peer in through a window to confirm once we get closer."

"It's a plan. And if we're caught?"

I thought quickly. "We say our van ran out of gas and ask the person inside if they have any."

Jamie nodded, her gaze never leaving the house. "Let's do this, then."

I jogged toward the building in front of me, ignoring the tremble in my limbs. When I was close enough, I darted toward the brick façade and pressed myself into the dented garage door. I cupped my hands over my eyes and peered into the dark space.

"It's empty," I told Jamie. All I could see were tools, an old tire, and a bike.

"What now?"

"Now we see if we can get a glimpse inside the house."

We moved around the edge of the house toward the back. The first window we came to had a shade pulled down, as did the second. As I walked, I listened for any telltale sign that someone occupied the space.

It was quiet. Totally quiet with no signs of life inside the house.

Was this all for nothing?

I didn't know. But I wouldn't leave without finding out.

I climbed onto the deck at the back of the house—a rickety one, at that—and peered inside. Jamie stayed right behind me, keeping lookout for anyone who might be nearby.

"What do you see?" she asked.

I squinted against the glare of the sun hitting the glass.

It was a living room with outdated furniture. A yellowed kitchen table could be seen at the edge of the space.

I squinted again and covered the sides of my eyes with my hands. What was that on the kitchen table?

"Anything?" Jamie asked.

"Jamie, I think I see some diabetes supplies on the table." Maybe this wasn't all for nothing.

"That might not mean anything," Jamie warned.

"I know. But it's something."

With more of a spring to my steps, I moved to the next set of windows. The kitchen. But I only saw more of the same.

Climbing from the deck, I moved toward the next windows. But a film covered them—not shades. They were the protective sheets of sticky paper you could put over the glass for privacy, like in a bathroom.

"It's weird," I muttered, staring at the gray and blue pebble design.

"What's weird?"

"It almost appears like the film is on the outside of the glass, between the actual window and the storm window."

"Why is that weird?"

"Because most people put the film on the inside of the window."

"Again, that doesn't necessarily mean anything." She looked away, still surveying everything around us.

"I know. I'm just observing. But if this film covers the rest of the windows, we're not going to learn much. I can't see anything through it."

"What are you suggesting?"

I turned toward my friend, my heart pounding furiously. "Plan B. I don't think anyone's home. But, just to be sure, I want to ring the doorbell."

"What will that prove?" Jamie's voice pitched higher.

"If someone is here, I want to know. Maybe we'll hear something."

"And if someone answers?"

"Then I go with my cover story about running out of gas."

Jamie nodded slowly, obviously not overly eager to jump into my plan of action. Finally, she said, "Okay, let's do it. Like I said, what do we have to lose, other than our lives?"

"Precisely." My voice sounded light, but I knew death was no laughing matter. Still, you had to keep your wits about you in these situations.

We walked to the front door. I kept my pace steady, trying to look normal instead of frenzied. I did glance over my shoulder, just to make sure no cars were pulling into the drive. Everything was clear.

After sucking in a deep breath to compose myself, I rang the bell. I heard it chiming inside the house, a dated little jingle that reminded me of my dad's grandfather clock.

Then we waited.

And waited.

Nothing.

I rang the bell again.

Again, nothing.

It looked like this was another dead end. I needed to come up with Plan C, apparently.

"At least we tried." Jamie took a step back. "I don't think there's anything we can do here—other than breaking in. The second time we may not be as lucky as the first."

I didn't move from the porch. Not yet, at least. Instead, I stood there, fighting rising frustration. I'd really thought this was going to be something. I still thought that. But I didn't know how to proceed.

Jamie tugged my arm, and I begrudgingly took a step back.

Just as my foot hit the top step, a sound caught my ear, and I froze. "Did you hear that?"

Jamie's eyebrows knit together in confusion. "Hear what?"

I put a hand over my lips. "Listen."

We both froze. *Please, do it again. Make the sound.*

But it was silent.

Had I been hearing things?

"Holly—"

Before Jamie could finish her sentence, the noise sounded again. She shut her mouth, and her eyes widened.

There it was. A tapping sound. Coming from one of the windows.

Someone *was* inside. And he or she was trying to get our attention.

CHAPTER 34

"MAYBE IT'S A TRAP," Jamie blurted.

"I don't see how." I rushed closer toward the sound, toward one of those windows that had been covered up with the sticky film. I shoved a garden reel—a boxy one—beneath the window and boosted myself up.

"What are you doing? Are you crazy?"

"Someone's in there." I reached for the window. Using all my strength, I shoved the storm window up with a screech that made my nerves wind even tighter.

The tapping sounded louder, faster.

I reached for the film and tried to find the edge. The covering clung tightly to the glass, though.

"Holly . . ." Jamie's voice held warning, but I couldn't stop now.

I had to know what was making the sound.

Finally, I found a corner of the plastic sheet. Using my fingernail, I pried it up until I was able to get a grasp on it. I peeled it back, feeling like this was some kind of sick Christmas present reveal.

My heart pounded out of control. What—who—was I going to see on the other side?

I braced myself for what I might find.

As I moved closer to the glass to see, something flew into the window.

I jumped back.

No, not some*thing*.

Some*one*.

I gulped in deep breaths of air as I waited. As my brain tried to process.

Then my vision cleared.

It was Avril, I realized.

Avril was inside the house. Knocking on the window.

And she looked terrified.

"We've got to get inside," I told Jamie. "And we need to call the police."

"My phone is jammed," Jamie said, still staring at the screen.

"What?" I glanced back at her as I tried to pick the lock to the front door. My pulse was pounding out of control, and I prayed I didn't have another episode. But I knew my blood pressure was high.

All I could do was fight it and pray. Pray hard.

"I don't know what's going on. I don't have a signal, though, which is weird because I have a great plan where I always have a signal."

"Keep trying. Maybe it's just a glitch."

"I will." Her fingers hit her phone again, tapping quickly as her frown remained.

Meanwhile, I continued to work the picks in the lock. My hands trembled so badly that it was taking longer than I wanted.

The tapping continued. If I looked out the corner of my eye, I could see Avril, still at the window, still looking at me with those wide, scared eyes.

I had no idea what was going on here. Well, maybe an idea. But I still had so many unanswered questions. I just needed to know that these girls were safe. And by these girls, I was assuming Sarah was here also.

"No, I don't have a signal," Jamie muttered, frustration rising in her voice. "It makes no sense."

"Maybe if you walk toward the woods? Maybe this is a dead zone."

"I'll try." She stepped off the porch, searching for the elusive signal on her phone screen.

We definitely needed backup here. I hoped Colerain had gotten my message.

I'd just seen Dr. Marks at his house. Did he go back to work? Would he head here? Was he working with someone else?

I had no idea of the answers to any of those questions. I just knew I was stepping into a potentially deadly situation. I was in over my head.

And I didn't say that very often, unless I knew it was absolutely true.

Finally, I heard the click I'd been waiting for. With baited breath, I straightened. Stuck my tool kit back into my skirt pocket. Then I twisted the handle.

The door opened. Relief flushed through me.

"Jamie!" I called.

She was still holding her phone in the air and had that frustrated look on her face. She slid it back into her pocket and rushed toward me. "Still no signal. I don't know what's going on. Maybe this place is like *The Twilight Zone*."

"Let's get in and get out as quickly as we can then."

"If you say so."

I stepped into the house and glanced around again. No one was in sight.

Wasting no more time, I rushed toward the hallway where I assumed the bedroom was located.

Several locks were installed on the door. What?

It was obviously designed to keep someone inside.

The bad feeling in my gut grew even worse. I didn't know what was going on, but I didn't like it. Not one bit.

With trembling hands, I turned the first lock. Twisted the second. Unlatched the third.

The door flew open, and Avril scrambled out. A gag was over her mouth, and her hands were bound behind her.

What in the world . . . ?

Jamie rushed toward her and took the gag from around her head. "Are you okay?"

Avril shook her head. "We've got to get out of here. Now! Before he gets back. He'll kill us all."

My blood felt colder at her words. "Is Sarah here?"

"Next room."

I rushed down the hallway, undid the locks, and opened the door.

Sarah stood there, bound like Avril. Tears popped into my eyes when I saw her. I threw my arms around her, holding her close—but only for a minute. Then I pulled her gag off.

"Are you okay, Wonder Girl?" I began working the ties around her wrists.

"I'm so glad you found me, Ms. Holly. I knew you would." Her voice cracked with desperation, and moisture streamed down her cheeks.

My gaze briefly traveled behind her. The room was

barren, other than a hospital bed, an IV line, and a lone teddy bear on the mattress.

My heart pounded at the sight. Something was wrong with the doctor. Very wrong.

"We'll have time to talk later," I told Sarah. "We've got to get you out of here now. Is there anyone else here?"

She shook her head. "Not that I know of. Just me and Avril."

I finished undoing the binds at her hands. "Do you feel okay?"

"I'm . . . I'm okay, Ms. Holly."

I swallowed down my emotions, took her arm, and led her into the hallway. Jamie and Avril were waiting for us there.

"We need to get out of here," I repeated. "Now."

We all took off toward the front door.

But as we reached it, someone stepped inside.

Dr. Marks.

With a gun.

We were five minutes too late.

CHAPTER 35

I RAISED my hands in the air, hoping to deescalate the situation. "I just want to get these girls to safety."

Dr. Marks snarled, his nostrils flaring and his teeth bared. "That's not a good idea. I'm not done yet."

"Dr. Marks, we can leave right now. We don't have to tell anyone about any of this." I moved in front of Sarah, trying my best to shield her.

She latched onto my arm behind me, and I could feel her trembling. It made the whole situation seem even more dire.

"That's not going to happen." He raised his gun higher. "Now I have to figure out what to do with you two. You've been a big complication in my plans. Everything was running so smoothly—until you started caring a little too much, Ms. Paladin. You weren't supposed to care. Don't you understand that?"

"No, I don't understand," I said, trying to buy time. "What plan are you talking about?"

His nostrils flared again, and the gun trembled in his hands. "I'm on the edge of discovering a cure for Type 1 diabetes. I just needed a few people to test it on. The FDA put a halt to my research with the Bayview Project, so I had to take matters into my own hands. I'm so close."

"There are better ways to do things." I still stared at his gun with dread. One move—one muscle-jerk reaction —and I could be dead. Jamie could be dead. Sarah. Avril.

"No, there aren't better ways to do things!" he yelled. "There are no other options. Don't you understand? No one understands. People are so feebleminded, they can't see past themselves and their own agendas."

"Why don't you explain it to me?" I glanced around, looking for something I could use as a weapon. There was nothing. No lamps. No paperweights. Letter openers. My best bet right now was a pillow, and that didn't seem very effective.

"They said my research wasn't safe. I went to talk to the Evans family—"

"Who are they?" I asked, wondering what I'd missed.

"They were the family who funded the research. They said I got violent with them, and they threatened to cut off the funding if I wasn't let go. I wasn't violent. I was passionate. There's a difference."

He probably thought he was being passionate right now also. I didn't say that thought aloud, though. "Ouch. That couldn't have felt good. I mean, if you discovered the cure, then you could stop other families from the suffering the way you did."

His eyes widened but still retained the off-balance look. "Exactly! My Zoe died. She shouldn't have. After she was gone, my wife and I couldn't handle it anymore. We blamed each other—resented each other—and eventually it led to our divorce. My job was all I had, and I needed to make a difference. They didn't understand how close I was."

"Maybe you could make them understand." I used my best counseling voice, trying to appease the man long enough to get everyone to safety.

"That's what I'm trying to do! I just need proof. Avril and Sarah are helping me find this proof."

"You're testing the drug out on them?" My stomach squeezed at the thought. *Lab rats.* That was what Sarah had told Cameron.

"That's right. And it's working. Isn't it, girls?" Dr. Marks looked at them with crazy eyes.

Both Avril and Sarah nodded, as if they were too frightened to do anything else but agree.

"Just let them go," I said. "You've done your tests. It's time to move on."

"I'm not finished yet! Can't you see that? These things can't be rushed."

I was going to have to make a move—and soon. The doctor was coming unhinged. And I sensed that there was no way I could talk him into letting us go.

I was the one who'd gotten Jamie and me into this. And I was the one responsible for Sarah. So it only made sense that I was the one who took a risk here.

"This is over, Dr. Marks." My voice shook. "You can't use these girls for your experiment."

"No one was supposed to notice them! Foster kids fall through the cracks all the time."

"That doesn't mean they're not important or that you can do whatever you want with them."

"I'm so close to figuring this out. Why'd you have to come here? Couldn't you just let it be?" The words sounded like a snarl.

"No, because I made Sarah a promise that I'd always watch out for her. Promises are everything. Why did you come back to get Sarah's diabetes meds?"

"I didn't come back."

"Then who did?"

He started to say something but stopped. He was working with someone, I realized. Who?

"I had to make it look like she left on her own," he

said. "Especially when you started asking so many questions."

"And my car tires? Did you slash them?"

"I don't have time for trivial things like that! Don't you see? But we had to slow you down."

We. He'd said we. What was I missing here? Who could be working with him?

I didn't have time to figure it out now.

He raised his gun higher again. "I need you all to go back down the hallway and into the bedrooms. Now. I need time to figure out what to do with you."

That wasn't going to happen.

"You should put the gun down," I told him, not moving. "We can talk this out."

"There's no talking this out! I've got to get the proof my new therapy works. Don't you understand?"

"I understand how important this is to you. But there are better ways."

"There's no other way! Now move!" Dr. Marks pointed with his gun toward the hallway.

A knot of anxiety formed in my stomach.

But I knew what I had to do.

Besides, my days might be limited anyway. More limited than the average person. Especially if those test results came back like I figured they would.

Before I could change my mind, I charged toward the doctor. "Jamie, run! To the van! Get the girls out of here."

Jamie froze behind me before bursting into action. I heard movement behind me as I fought for my life.

I tackled the doctor.

We collided together on the floor. Wrestled.

I had to get that gun away from him.

I had to make sure the girls were gone and safe.

But I was no match for the doctor. I knew I wouldn't be. He was stronger and bigger than me.

He thrashed on the floor, fighting me off.

And then, in the midst of our struggle, the gun went off.

CHAPTER 36

I FROZE, wondering if I'd been shot. But I felt no pain.

Not yet, at least.

I looked down at the doctor. His face was twisted, and he grabbed his knee.

I pulled myself off him. Spotted his gun on the floor beside his hand. Grabbed it before he could.

Then I gave him a once-over.

His leg.

He'd shot himself in the leg.

With labored breathing, I stood and backed away.

"Look what you've done!" he yelled.

I gasped in deep gulps of air, trying to get my body under control. But adrenaline still coursed through me and made my entire body feel wired and jerky.

At that moment, cars pulled up outside. I saw them through the open front door.

The police.

They were here.

I still held that gun, just in case the doctor made a sudden move. But he acted like he was in too much pain to do that.

Chase rushed through the door. Glanced at me. Then glanced at the doctor.

Without saying anything, he pulled the man up and handcuffed him, despite his protests. He handed Dr. Marks off to another officer to read him his rights before coming toward me and carefully taking the gun from my hands. "Are you okay, Holly?"

I nodded, but I could feel the shock claiming my body. "The girls . . ."

"They're outside. They're okay. An ambulance is behind us, and the paramedics will check them out."

I swallowed hard and let my gaze lock on his. "I didn't think you were coming."

"Colerain didn't get the message until late. That whole thing was a bad idea. You call me whenever you need something. You know I'll always answer. I don't know what I was thinking."

I nodded again. "I know you will."

"Holly?" He stooped his head down, his gaze filled with worry.

Without another word, I fell into his arms. I let him hug me. Hold me. Make me feel like no one would ever get to me again.

And I cried. I cried hard. I cried for Sarah. I cried for myself. I cried for Dr. Marks even—cried because his grief had led him to these extremes.

I even cried for Drew. For Chase. For my utter confusion about my life.

I liked to think I had everything together. But the older I got, the more I realized how little I knew. And areas that had seemed so black-and-white were suddenly feeling gray.

I had to make some serious decisions.

"We have a lot to talk about," Chase murmured into the top of my head.

"Yes, we do. We really do."

The crime-scene crew had arrived at the house and were sweeping it for any evidence left behind—and apparently, there was plenty, with all the medical supplies there.

Chase had taken all of us back to the hospital. Jamie and I had been given coffee. The girls had been admitted, and they appeared to be doing okay.

But Chase needed to talk to them, and he was starting with Sarah.

While Jamie talked to Colerain, I sat beside Sarah's bed and held her hand, so grateful she was okay. So, so grateful.

Thank You, Jesus!

"How did this all begin, Sarah?" Chase asked.

"It started when I got a message from the school office from Dr. Marks. He said he needed to see me and that Holly had said it was okay. It was time-sensitive to my disease." Sarah shook her head. "I know that sounds crazy, but he was my doctor. I didn't think he'd lie."

"So he picked you up?" I asked.

Sarah nodded. "Yeah, I thought it really must be time-sensitive for him to go out of his way to do that."

"I thought a woman picked you up?" I asked. Something wasn't making sense. The office would have had a record of that message coming in.

Unless it hadn't come in.

Unless someone had made that message up to lure Sarah outside.

Maybe that someone was the other person Dr. Marks had been working with.

Sarah shrugged. "Why would you think a woman was picking me up?"

"Because Ms. Baldwin said that's what she saw."

Sarah frowned, looking entirely too tiny and frail in that hospital bed. "Ms. Baldwin wasn't there when I got in his car. I did pass her in the hallway on my way out. I

RANDOM ACTS OF OUTRAGE

was on autopilot, going to meet you out front. But when I passed her, she reminded me about the note and encouraged me to see the doctor. Told me I had to be careful with my health problems."

"Ms. Baldwin?" Wait . . . I exchanged a glance with Chase.

But he was already on his phone, sending someone over to her place.

She must have been in this with the doctor the whole time. Had she changed facts to throw us off her trail? Had she kept an eye on the situation for the doctor when he was at work?

That was how it appeared. She was the second part of Dr. Marks's "we" statement—his foot soldier, so to speak.

"He gave Avril and me these injections. He called it stem-cell therapy," Sarah continued. "Honestly, I did feel better after the doses. Except he kept us locked in those rooms."

"But you called me," I said. "How did you do that?"

"He didn't know I had the phone," she said. "Sorry about that, by the way. I knew I shouldn't have kept it from you."

"We'll talk about it later. But did Dr. Marks call you? Did he get your number?"

"No, Ms. Baldwin gave me that message in class. Said the call came into the office."

"What?" How could I have been so stupid that I didn't see that?

"But then the doctor put some kind of cell-phone block on the house when he realized I'd called you. He got really paranoid and mad. He started putting the gags over our mouths. It was all my fault. I didn't realize what was happening soon enough."

"Why didn't you just tell me when you called what was going on?"

"I was afraid you wouldn't care," she started. "At least when I called the first time. The second time, I was afraid Dr. Marks would hear me. After he realized I had the phone, he made me leave that message on your Chatbook account before confiscating my cell."

"He thought of everything, I guess."

"Maybe. I just . . ." She shivered. "I thought I was going to die there, Ms. Holly."

I squeezed her hand more tightly. "You didn't. You're going to be okay."

"Do I get to come home with you?" She stared at me, her eyes hopeful.

"That's the plan, Sarah. But I think there's someone here to see you."

"To see me?" She raised her eyebrows.

I nodded and stood. Walking to the door, I found Lula outside. She rushed toward Sarah with tears in her eyes.

I'd called her on the way here. How could I not? Chase had said it was okay.

Sarah and Lula both cried and hugged. An officer remained stationed in the room as Chase led me into the hallway.

"Good work, Holly."

"Are you going to arrest me?"

"Not this time."

"But maybe next time?'

"I'm hoping there won't be a next time." He paused, his brief humor fading. "I need to go talk to Avril. Can you wait here?"

"I have nowhere to go." And no car—not until Jamie finished talking to Colerain, at least.

He nodded slowly, oceans of unspoken conversations between us.

Then I sat in one of the gray chairs outside Sarah's room and waited for more answers to come to light.

CHAPTER 37

LULA STEPPED out a few minutes later. "The doctor said Sarah needs to rest."

"I'm sure she does."

"Thank you for calling me."

"I would want to know if I was in your shoes."

She stood beside me, her expression tentative. "Holly, I want her to come live with me."

My heart both ached and rejoiced at her words. "I know you do. And I'm going to advocate for that. Until it happens, Sarah can stay with me."

"You mean it?" Tears welled in her eyes again.

"Yes, I mean it. I'll always be there for her too."

Lula threw her arms around me. "Thank you, Holly. Thank you so much."

Ten minutes after Lula left, Chase came back out and sat beside me.

"Good news," he started.

"I'd love some good news." Would. I. Ever.

"My officers brought Tam Baldwin in, and she confessed to her role in helping the doctor with his scheme."

I'd guess she'd been the hooded figure by my car as well. The tire slasher. Basically, she'd been the doctor's foot soldier. "How did they even know each other?"

"She used to work for him before she became a teacher. She believed in his cause. Her dad had diabetes, and she saw him suffer with that. She wanted to be an agent of change."

"Did she specifically work at the school with the hopes of befriending Sarah?"

"No, but they decided to target Sarah because Tam Baldwin was at the school. Her previous school, before she was transferred, just happened to be the school Avril attended."

"That's how they decided who should be their guinea pigs." I shook my head. "It's sad, really."

"It is. We're still looking into everything, Holly. We don't have all the answers yet."

"I know."

He shifted and his gaze darkened. "There is one other thing."

"What's that?" I could tell it wasn't good news.

"The third kid in foster care—George, the one who disappeared two years ago? We don't know what happened to him. He apparently ran away from the doctor."

"And he didn't go to the police?"

"No, he didn't. My guess is that he got out of town. Maybe found a life somewhere else. But we're still searching for him."

"At least he got away."

"At least." I'd pray for him and pray that he was found. No one should go through what these kids had. No one.

"Ms. Paladin," someone said beside me.

I looked up and saw Dr. Harris standing there. "Doctor."

Dread pooled in my stomach. This was it. I could sense it. The moment I'd find out the truth.

"I was just about to call you. Do you have a few minutes? We got those test results back."

"Yes, of course." I stood and pressed my hand against my skirt, ironing out imaginary wrinkles.

"Come to my office?"

I looked up, a sudden case of the jitters claiming my muscles. "Chase, would you—"

"Go with you?" He finished. "I'd be honored."

He kept his hand on my elbow as we walked down the hall. Inside Dr. Harris's office, Chase made sure I was seated in a chair before he lowered himself beside me.

Dr. Harris pulled out a folder and stared at it a moment. I couldn't read his expression. Was this bad news? Good news?

I had no idea.

"Like I said, we got the test results back," he still stared at the paper. "And . . ."

I held my breath, hardly able to wait.

"It looks like you have . . . anemia."

I blinked. "What?"

"It's true," Dr. Harris said. "It's what's making you feel so tired and light-headed. But if you start on a good multi-vitamin with iron, you should be good to go."

"That's it?" Certainly I hadn't heard correctly.

He smiled. "That's it. Everything else looks good. But you might want to manage your stress levels better."

"I'll do my best."

"Maybe your boyfriend here could take you out for a good steak dinner to celebrate," he continued, his smile wide. "That might help too."

I didn't bother to correct him. Instead, I left his office in a daze—a happy daze. Holly Anna Paladin, optimist extraordinaire, had been expecting the worst.

"That's great news, Holly." Chase turned toward me.

"It is. I'm . . . I'm thankful."

"Maybe you should get home now and rest. I've got things under control here."

"I can't go home without Sarah."

"I'm going to stay here with her. I promise she'll be okay. But you need to go home and catch your breath. Then you can come back. I'll have one of my officers take you."

"Are you sure she'll be okay?"

"I'm going to be questioning her some more. The social worker is also here. Then the doctors will want to see her again. You've got a good two hours before you're going to be able to go back in that room with her."

I nodded. "Okay, then. Maybe I will shower." It might make me feel more alive.

He squeezed my arm. "Good work, Holly."

"Thanks."

I had just enough time to shower and get changed when the doorbell rang.

Drew was here.

I'd called him and asked him to come over.

I smiled when he stepped inside and planted a soft kiss on my cheek.

"I have a feeling you haven't been resting," he said, tapping the tip of my nose playfully.

I wished I felt lighthearted and fun-loving. Right now, I was anything but. "I haven't been, unfortunately. Can we sit down?"

We took a seat on my couch, and I filled him in on the Sarah situation.

He gripped my hand. "I'm so glad she's been found, Holly."

"Me too."

He studied my face. "Is there something else you need to say?"

"There is." I let out a long breath, hating myself just a little for having this conversation. "Not long ago, I told Sarah that she had to be herself and let other people be themselves. Then, maybe if in the process of being who they were created to be they also found they could be friends, then she'd found something she could treasure forever and always."

"What?" He twisted his head with confusion.

Why did everyone do that when I brought up my theory? "I'm just saying that people should be themselves, and then the people who like them should be in their lives. Relationships should never be forced and people should never feel like they have to change in order to be accepted."

"I can agree with that."

"The thing is . . . I'm not sure I can be me being me when I'm with you being you."

Emotion washed across his face. Confusion. Regret. Sorrow? "I would never want you to be someone other than who you are, Holly."

"I know that. But to fit into your life, I . . . I don't feel like myself."

"I want you to be you, Holly. I feel like we're a great fit."

"And that's what makes all of this even harder. You see, the thing is, when I go to the funeral home to help you, I hate it."

"You do?" He sounded genuinely surprised.

I licked my lips. "It makes me feel like I'm reliving my dad's death all over. And . . . I just feel anxious, if I'm being honest."

"Like I said, Holly, what kind of man would I be if I asked you to be someone other than who you are?"

And it was statements like that that made this even harder. "And I deeply appreciate that."

Drew shifted, his grip on my hand loosening some. "What's the bottom line here?"

I licked my lips again, appreciating his directness. "Look, I was engaged to a guy who dropped me. And then I was engaged to Chase, and I dropped him. I don't want to be a serial fiancée or wishy-washy. And that's part of the reason why I keep hesitating to say I love you. I need to be sure before I make any promises."

"I want you to be sure also."

Drew was just so nice and considerate. I'd be a fool to walk away from him. But I had too many questions in my mind.

"I just need a little time," I finally said.

"What do you mean? Are we breaking up?" His voice sounded strained as the words left his lips.

"Like, 'I've got to figure my life out' time. And maybe that means breaking up or spending time apart or cooling it on the serious level. I don't know. I don't want to be a jerk."

"I'm not sure you could ever be a jerk."

"I just have to figure out what I really want."

He swallowed hard. "Does this have to do with Chase?"

I wanted to say no, but I couldn't. "I don't know. I've been in denial about my emotions, but I've realized that emotions are barometers of what's going on in our thought lives. I just . . . I just don't know. That's the most honest thing I can say."

"I understand." Drew stood. "I'll be here waiting for you when you realize that your future is better with me."

Emotions lodged in my throat. "Thank you, Drew."

"I'm going to give you some space now."

I let go of his hand and watched him walk away, wondering if I'd just made the dumbest choice ever.

But when he was gone, I hopped in my car and went to see Sarah.

I didn't know what the future held. I didn't know if it would be Chase or Drew. I didn't know how much longer Sarah would be with me or if I'd ever achieve my dream of becoming a mom. Every time I got closer, a new roadblock appeared.

But I had a life to live, and I didn't know how much time I had left to do that. It could be years. Or it could be days. None of us knew.

Reaching my dreams wasn't a sprint into bliss and happiness. No, reaching my dreams meant sweat and hard work and tears. It meant trying and failing. Questioning. But keeping my eye on the prize.

So, right now, I was going to put one foot in front of the other and move forward.

I was going to be me being me. And when I found someone who accepted me for me, then I'd have found the greatest gift of all.

ALSO BY CHRISTY BARRITT:

HOLLY ANNA PALADIN MYSTERIES:

When Holly Anna Paladin is given a year to live, she embraces her final days doing what she loves most—random acts of kindness. But when one of her extreme good deeds goes horribly wrong, implicating Holly in a string of murders, Holly is suddenly in a different kind of fight for her life. She knows one thing for sure: she only has a short amount of time to make a difference. And if helping the people she cares about puts her in danger, it's a risk worth taking.

THE SQUEAKY CLEAN MYSTERY
SERIES:

On her way to completing a degree in forensic science, Gabby St. Claire drops out of school and starts her own crime-scene cleaning business. When a routine cleaning job uncovers a murder weapon the police overlooked, she realizes that the wrong person is in jail. She also realizes that crime scene cleaning might be the perfect career for utilizing her investigative skills.

LANTERN BEACH MYSTERY SERIES:

You can take the detective out of the investigation, but you can't take the investigator out of the detective.

A notorious gang puts a bounty on Detective Cady Matthews's head after she takes down their leader, leaving her no choice but to hide until she can testify at trial. But her temporary home across the country on a remote North Carolina island isn't as peaceful as she initially thinks. Living under the new identity of Cassidy Livingston, she struggles to keep her investigative skills tucked away. When local police bungle numerous investigations, she can't resist stepping in. But Cassidy is supposed to be keeping a low profile. One wrong move could lead to both her discovery and her demise. Can she bring justice to the island . . . or will the hidden currents surrounding her pull her under for good?

THE WORST DETECTIVE EVER:

I'm not really a private detective. I just play one on TV.

Joey Darling, better known to the world as Raven Remington, detective extraordinaire, is trying to separate herself from her invincible alter ego. She played the spunky character for five years on the hit TV show *Relentless*, which catapulted her to fame and into the role of Hollywood's sweetheart. When her marriage falls apart, her finances dwindle to nothing, and her father disappears, Joey finds herself on the Outer Banks of North Carolina, trying to piece together her life away from the limelight. But as people continually mistake her for the character she played on TV, she's tasked with solving real life crimes . . . even though she's terrible at it.

ABOUT THE AUTHOR

USA Today has called Christy Barritt's books "scary, funny, passionate, and quirky."

Christy writes both mystery and romantic suspense novels that are clean with underlying messages of faith. Her books have won the Daphne du Maurier Award for Excellence in Suspense and Mystery, have been twice nominated for the Romantic Times Reviewers' Choice Award, and have finaled for both a Carol Award and Foreword Magazine's Book of the Year.

She is married to her Prince Charming, a man who thinks she's hilarious—but only when she's not trying to be. Christy is a self-proclaimed klutz, an avid music lover who's known for spontaneously bursting into song, and a road trip aficionado.

When she's not working or spending time with her family, she enjoys singing, playing the guitar, and exploring small, unsuspecting towns where people have no idea how accident-prone she is.

Find Christy online at:
www.christybarritt.com
www.facebook.com/christybarritt
www.twitter.com/cbarritt

Sign up for Christy's newsletter to get information on all of her latest releases here: **www.christybarritt.com/newsletter-sign-up/**

If you enjoyed this book, please consider leaving a review.

Made in the USA
Las Vegas, NV
25 July 2024

92883861R00189